A MODERATE CHANCE OF SCREAMING

CASSIAN R. ROWE

A MODERATE CHANCE OF SCREAMING

RAVEN ROW PRESS

Published by Raven Row Press

© 2026 Cassian R. Rowe
The right of Cassian R. Rowe to be identified as the Author of this Work has been asserted by them in accordance with the Copyright, Designs and Patents Act 1988.

All rights reserved. No part of this publication may be reproduced, stored in a retrieval system, or transmitted in any form or by any means—electronic, mechanical, photocopying, recording, or otherwise—without prior written permission of the publisher, except in the case of brief quotations embodied in critical reviews or articles.

This is a work of fiction. Names, characters, places, and incidents are the product of the author's imagination or are used fictitiously. Any resemblance to actual persons, living or dead, events, or locales is purely coincidental.

Cover art by Artwerkz Gallery
Interior layout and formatting by Studio Pedroza

First edition: 2026
ISBN (Paperback): 978-1-7345271-7-9

Printed and published in the United States of America.

For permissions, inquiries, or bulk orders, please contact:
Raven Row Press
ravenrow@akopublishing.com

For anyone who ever felt like a character in
their own chaotic story.
And to the gin, for its invaluable contribution
to my writing.

CHAPTER ONE

ONE TOO MANY DAGGERS AND JUST ENOUGH ALE

D EADGOAT HOLLOW WASN'T KNOWN FOR its hospitality.
The village sat tucked into a crooked fold of the hills, where the trees grew thick and gnarled, and the sky seemed perpetually smothered by heavy clouds. Few came here by choice, and even fewer stayed longer than necessary. It was the kind of place where a traveller's footsteps might quicken and then falter under the weight of unspoken warnings in the air.

Moss clung to the stone walls of its ramshackle buildings, and the crooked chimneys puffed sluggish smoke that smelled of burnt pine and old bones. More than once, locals muttered about the Hollow's history: about lost miners, old curses, and the blood that still stained the soil beneath the mud-caked streets.

It was not a place for dreams or lighthearted laughter.
And yet, on the edge of that forsaken place stood one refuge, a sanctuary from the judgemental eyes outside, even

though it was more tavern in name than in actual comfort.

The Staggering Sow.

A ramshackle tavern squeezed between a butcher's shop that still smelled faintly of fresh meat and a blacksmith whose hammering never ceased from dawn until dusk. Its windows were smeared with grime, the wood beneath the scrawled sign was splintered and warped, and the air inside was thick with the smells of spilt ale, smoke, and too many secrets whispered beneath ragged breath. The ale was warm, the floors were sticky, and the house special was either stew or rat, depending on the size of the bones.

But for men like Adanion Moonshadow and Kril of the Stonetooth Clan, the Hollow's one tavern offered two undeniable selling points: It stayed open late, and it didn't ask questions.

For them, this meant more than just hours to drink. It was a place where stories could be swapped without fear, where debts could be paid with a grin, and where silence could be a shield from a world that never stopped grinding. That was more than enough.

The tavern creaked with every shift of the wind outside. Rain pattered lazily against the grimy windows, and the heavy scent of spilt beer, wet cloaks, and pipe smoke hung in the air like a tired old ghost.

Inside, the low murmur of conversation was punctuated by the occasional thud of a tankard hitting the table or the scrape of a chair against the worn floorboards. Candles guttered in wrought-iron holders, casting shadows that danced and flickered like restless spirits.

The hearth fire was the room's reluctant heart, a stubborn blaze that refused to die despite the damp that crept through every crack. It spluttered and hissed, sending sparks up the chimney in a weak salute to the storm outside.

At the table nearest the hearth, Adanion lounged back in his chair, boots crossed on the table, a wine glass balanced with careless elegance. His thick, tousled silver hair caught the torchlight like moonlight on water. His features were sharp, his mouth too quick to smirk, and his eyes flicked like coin: bright, clever, and slightly dangerous.

A dark, worn cloak hung from his shoulders, hinting at coin but not inviting questions. He wore his confidence like a second shirt: easy, tailored, and slightly smug. His surname, Moonshadow, was merely a convenient translation of the complex Aevrinai name, Liraevalen—a name he used only for running from bailiffs and other legal unpleasantness. It wasn't arrogance, exactly, more the assurance of someone who'd lied to kings, kissed assassins, and walked away smiling from both.

He unfolded like a story best read after dark, every movement precise, every tilt of his head revealing the gentle taper of his pointed ears, the unmistakable grace of an Aevrinai in motion. His eyes always scanned for exits, weighing glances, as if he always had a plan, or at least a good excuse.

Across the table, the barmaid giggled as he whispered something in her ear. She was blushing. Adanion was smirking.

It was a familiar scene.

She had brown eyes, the colour of syrup left too long in a sunlit jar, and freckles sprinkled like cinnamon across her cheeks. Her apron was stained from long hours of work, but she leaned in like this was the most interesting conversation she'd had all week. Adanion's hand rested lightly on hers; not possessive, just enough to suggest that if the world were simpler, he might have stayed.

Behind him, Kril drank mead straight from a cask-sized

mug, arms thick as oak beams resting on the table's edge. Half Hryndahl, his frame still massive, took up more space than the bench allowed, forcing the wood to groan in protest. Scar-laced arms bulged beneath the rough fur of his sleeveless vest, and his freshly shorn scalp glistened in the hearthlight, marked by a single old war tattoo that curved behind one ear like a half-forgotten oath.

His face was broad and blunt, carved more for enduring punches than delivering compliments. A heavy beard, bristling and black with sparse threads of silver, framed his mouth, a mouth rarely used for words, and even less for smiling. He looked like a siege engine that had learned to walk upright.

His axe, Lorna, leaned beside him: half his height, double his weight, and notched like it had strong opinions. The haft was wrapped in worn leather, darkened with sweat and age, and the blade had a slight tilt to it, like it wanted to leap into trouble uninvited. He'd named her years ago after the first woman who broke his heart—and the only one who'd ever tried to kill him with a skillet. Lorna hadn't survived the encounter. The skillet had. He kept it in his pack.

'You're doing that thing again,' Kril grunted, not looking up from his drink.

He spoke with the gravelly patience of someone who had seen too much and slept too little. His voice rarely rose above a growl unless absolutely necessary, usually just before something needed breaking. Though he kept his gaze on the froth circling his mead, Kril didn't need to look to know exactly what his companion was doing.

He'd seen the look too many times: the lean forward, the lazy grin, the precise level of attentiveness that suggested deep interest without ever fully committing. It was Adanion's version of baiting a trap, only his snares weren't made of wire or twine: just charm, timing, and the occasional well-placed compliment.

'What thing?' Adanion didn't turn around.

He already knew what Kril meant. It wasn't the first time they'd had this conversation, and it wouldn't be the last. Still, the Aevrinai's tone was innocent enough to almost sound genuine.

'The smouldering. You smoulder when you want something.'

'I want a lot of things,' Adanion replied smoothly, swirling his wine. 'But mostly I want her name. Possibly intimate knowledge of what she looks like without the apron. And maybe a few more refills.'

Kril glanced up just long enough to snort into his drink. It was a small miracle that the table hadn't yet collapsed beneath his weight, but then again, it had probably been reinforced, likely for his benefit.

'Keep it up,' Kril said, wiping foam from his beard, 'and someone's going to stab you again.'

It wasn't a threat: just a prediction. One rooted in experience. The last time Adanion had tried his luck with a war widow and a loaded dice game in Rivertown, he'd ended the night missing a boot and bleeding from just above the hip.

Adanion glanced down at the faint scar just above his hip, barely visible beneath the linen shirt.

'Worth it.'

The response came with a soft smile, not for Kril but for the memory itself. Even pain could be poetic in hindsight, if you'd lived through enough of it.

'That one's got a dagger in each boot,' Adanion murmured, wineglass raised. 'And another in the back of his belt.

Overcompensating, or just indecisive?'

Conversation in the tavern stuttered and stalled. Chairs scraped. Someone coughed too loudly.

Adanion didn't flinch.

'And that,' he said quietly, eyes still fixed on the serving girl, 'is the sound of a man trying to be clever in boots too tight.'

Adanion's eyes flicked across the room. A wiry man in a patched green cloak was slinking towards the bar, trying not to look like he was watching them. Unfortunately for him, he was doing a terrible job of it.

'New face. Walks like he's got a secret and a rash,' Adanion continued, voice low, amused. 'Think he's here for us?'

Kril didn't look. He just took another sip.

'Too many daggers,' he muttered.

Adanion stood. 'Honestly, if you're going to come into a tavern smelling of desperation and cheap steel, at least do us the courtesy of falling with style.'

The man froze. Looked up. Tried a smile. Failed.

Adanion stepped closer, boots soft on the sticky floorboards. The firelight caught the glint of rings on his fingers: not gaudy, just enough to hint at wealth or theft, and the slight curve of a dagger now in his hand, seemingly conjured from nowhere.

'I'm going to give you a choice,' he said, voice low and polite. 'Walk out now with your daggers and your dignity, or stay and find out how many limbs you get to keep.'

A long pause.

Then the man stood, muttered something about a mistake, and made a brisk exit, without his ale, but with all his limbs.

Adanion watched the door swing shut behind him.

'Overcompensating,' he said, sheathing the dagger. 'Definitely not indecisive.'

He turned back to Kril and sank into his chair like nothing had happened.

'Now. Where were we? Ah yes: smouldering.'

A heavy gust of wind slammed the tavern door open with a bang. Heads turned. A few hands moved subtly towards hilts. The locals of the Hollow didn't like surprises, and they especially didn't trust wind.

The wind was cold and wet and somehow seemed personal. It dragged in with it the scent of far-off places, of steel and earth and something that made the old hound by the hearth whimper and tuck its nose under one paw.

Chairs creaked. Dice stilled mid-roll. Even the bard in the corner missed a note on his lute. The fire popped as if trying to back away itself.

She stepped in like she owned the place—and from the silence that followed, no one dared suggest otherwise.

Tall. Green-skinned. Her leather armour clung like a second skin, worn to the shape of her body by long rides and long nights. Every curve it followed looked like a decision, not an accident. The dark armour bore an uncommon finish: polished and marked with faint patterns that caught the light; ancient and nearly forgotten, known to a select few.

An orc.

Not the 'grunting cave-dweller' kind. No, this one had eyes like molten amber and a smirk that played along a strong, angular jaw that promised either death or something much more interesting.

Two wicked-looking axes were strapped to her back. And a walk that said she'd cut down anyone who so much as looked at her sideways, and then take their drink for the trouble.

Her voice hadn't spoken yet, but somehow you could already hear it: low, rough velvet over sharpened steel. The kind of voice that made promises with bite marks.

A silver ring pierced one eyebrow. Black warpaint traced the line of her jaw, not as decoration, but as tradition: hers, not yours. Her boots left muddy prints as she crossed the floor, each step a quiet threat. Every man who watched her wanted to run, fight, or marry her, and some looked ready to try all three.

There was a roughness to her stillness, like she was always listening for something behind her. Not fear, just habit, carved deep.

Her axes didn't jangle when she moved. She moved like someone who'd learned long ago that noise gets you killed.

And beneath the leather and steel, she carried something heavier: the weight of too many names, none of them hers.

Kril choked a little on his mead. Adanion raised one elegant brow.

'She's trouble,' Kril muttered.

'She's perfect,' Adanion replied.

There was admiration in his voice, but not just for her looks. It was the way she moved: purposeful, controlled, like a blade freshly whetted and unsheathed. She had presence, and not the rehearsed kind that Adanion used at court or around noblewomen. Hers was real. Earned. Dangerous.

The orc woman stalked past tables, ignoring the staring patrons. A dwarven merchant fumbled his drink. A rogue sitting near the hearth coughed into his mug, trying to look indifferent. One of the locals tried to whistle and failed halfway through.

No one in the Staggering Sow liked to be reminded that there were bigger predators in the woods, and this one had just walked into their den, unbothered and unimpressed.

She passed a table of sellswords who were loudly arguing over a game of bone dice. One of them, broad-shouldered and foolish, opened his mouth to make a comment. Then her gaze slid his way, slow and sharp as a whetted axe. The words died on his tongue. He suddenly found the grain of the table very interesting.

Even the barkeep, a scarred man with knuckles like boulders and a perpetual sneer, kept polishing the same mug without looking up. His eyes flicked once towards the newcomer, then down to the mug again. No trouble, his body said. Not tonight.

She reached the job board, an old slab of splintered oak covered in crumpled flyers and bloodstained bounty posters, and drove a dagger into it with a casual flick of her wrist. The blade sank clean to the hilt.

The parchment fluttered slightly as it settled.

It wasn't the first time a dagger had been lodged in that board. But it might've been the first time no one made a joke about it. The impact echoed too loudly in the quiet tavern, and even the bard in the corner paused before cautiously plucking another string.

Gold foil lettering caught the firelight, shimmering beneath a layer of rainwater droplets, advertising: *Wanted: Discreet adventurers for a high-risk extraction. Great reward. Moderate chance of screaming.*

It was the shimmer that got Adanion's attention first: not the blade, not the sudden silence, but the glint of gold script like the flash of a promise. He was on his feet before Kril finished his mug.

'Let me guess,' Kril muttered, rising reluctantly and grabbing his axe. 'We're getting stabbed tonight.'

Adanion grinned, finishing his wine in one smooth motion and setting the glass down without looking.

'Only if we're lucky.'

He was already halfway to the board before Kril finished standing. The elf moved like a whisper in moonlight: elegant, effortless, and just annoying enough to make everyone else feel clumsy by comparison.

The movement was unconscious, but deliberate. He straightened his shoulders just a touch. Let the wine-sheen in his eyes be replaced by the glitter of mischief. He walked not just towards the job but towards something else: possibility, perhaps. Or fate. Or maybe just another opportunity to get in over his head with a woman who looked like she bathed in blood and laughed at curses.

The tavern seemed to part for him. Drunken mercenaries leaned aside without realising they were doing it. A gnome in a stained cloak blinked twice and dropped his cards. Even the old Faeluran sleeping in the corner cracked open one yellow eye as Adanion passed, murmuring something in a language that was probably either prophetic or just cursed.

Adanion reached the job board just as the parchment stopped fluttering. He didn't touch it immediately, just stood there, reading the gold foil lettering as if it were a poem written just for him.

The message wasn't long, but it said all it needed. Not a name. Not a signature. Just the glint of coin, danger, and intrigue. And that was more than enough.

'Discreet adventurers,' he murmured to himself. 'How very flattering.'

He could feel eyes on him. Not the eyes of the crowd, who'd returned to their drinks and whispers, but her eyes. He didn't have to turn to know. The weight of her gaze was solid.

Heavy. Measured.

Then he turned.

The orc had ordered a drink: black rum, neat, no hesitation, and now leaned casually with one elbow resting atop the bar, watching Adanion with the kind of look usually reserved for game animals and bad ideas. Her smirk deepened.

Adanion gave her the same smile he'd once used on a duchess, two countesses, and a rather spirited priestess of the Moonmaiden. 'Lovely handwriting,' he said. 'Yours?'

'No,' she said—slow, low, and dark with promise—one that invited trouble and whispered of secrets worth chasing. 'The blood was mine. The words were someone else's.'

Her tone was dry, matter-of-fact, but her eyes were watching him closely, calculating. Testing. She wasn't just gauging his wit. She was weighing something deeper: the way he stood, the way he smiled, the way he didn't flinch at her answer. He passed the first test, barely.

'I find collaboration so underrated.'

She chuckled, a sound that could've melted glaciers or split skulls, depending on her mood. 'You're quick.'

Adanion bowed slightly, never breaking eye contact. 'And yet somehow, I always have time for Orcish royalty.'

'You think I'm royalty?'

'I think anyone who walks into a place like this, pins up a job, and doesn't get immediately stabbed must have some kind of divine right.'

It was more than flattery. It was truth, wrapped in velvet and served with a smirk. Adanion had met all sorts in his travels: kings, warlords, self-styled barons, but very few carried themselves like this orc did. She wasn't here to prove anything. She was here because she belonged.

'I am Orzhaan,' she said, the word a low growl that cut his smile in half. She took a long drink from her rum and didn't look away. 'You talk too much.'

'Better than brooding silently,' Adanion replied. 'Trust me, I've tried. People just assume I'm constipated.'

That earned the faintest twitch of amusement at the corner of her mouth, and her eyes narrowed: not in suspicion, but in something closer to interest.

Kril finally caught up, ducking beneath the ceiling beam with the ease of someone who'd hit it many, many times before. He stopped beside Adanion and crossed his arms. The floor creaked beneath him in protest.

He didn't speak right away. Just stood there, evaluating the situation in the way only a man who'd been dragged into far too many of Adanion's schemes could. One look at the orc. One glance at the job board. A long sigh followed.

'She giving us the job, or killing us for sport?' he asked.

The orc tilted her head. 'Depends. Can you carry things without complaining?'

'Yes,' Kril said.

'No,' Adanion said at the same time.

She raised an eyebrow. 'Which one's lying?'

Kril shrugged. 'We take turns.'

There was a beat of silence, not awkward, but filled with unspoken calculations. The orc's eyes flicked between them: tall and quiet, sharp and clever. One with a body like a siege weapon. The other with a tongue like a dagger. She'd seen worse teams. She'd hired worse.

The barmaid from earlier reappeared with another round, casting a quick glance at the orc before setting the tray down with practised care. Her hands trembled just slightly, though she tried to hide it. Adanion offered her a wink that earned him a poorly hidden smile before she scurried off again.

There was something in her smile that held no illusions. Not adoration, just a brief wish that she were brave enough to live the kind of lives these mad bastards seemed to walk into.

'So,' Adanion said, lifting the rum glass but not drinking it. 'This extraction: something tells me we won't be liberating a misplaced chicken.'

The orc snorted into her drink, then tilted her head, amused despite herself. He was irreverent. But he wasn't wasting her time.

'No,' the orc replied. 'Vault job. Old empire ruins. Traps, mercenaries, maybe something cursed if we're lucky.'

'Cursed if we're lucky,' Kril repeated. 'Why do people keep saying that like it's good?'

He said it to the room more than anyone in particular, but the orc chuckled again, just once, and it sounded dangerously close to approval.

Adanion was still staring at her. 'And what are we extracting?'

She reached into her cloak and produced a small, iron coin. It was warped, pitted with age, and etched with a strange symbol: half sun, half skull.

The firelight flickered across its surface, catching in the grooves like blood pooling in old scars. It was the kind of object that didn't just look ancient, it felt ancient. Like it had been buried in forgotten catacombs, listening to the dead whisper secrets for centuries.

Adanion leaned closer, intrigued. 'That's—'

'Classified,' she interrupted. She didn't offer the coin for inspection, merely holding it up, her thumb rubbing the symbol. 'This is simply proof of my seriousness.' Her hand closed over the coin with a soft click of leather on metal. It vanished beneath her fitted leather armour, slipped into a thin, sewn pouch that lay flat against her ribs, with the same smooth finality as a blade sheathed. She didn't need to say more. The image was burned into both their minds.

Kril looked at Adanion. 'Do we like classified?'

'We love classified.'

'I like punching things.'

'We love that too.'

The orc nodded once, and pushed off the bar. 'Midnight. Old shrine on the west ridge. Bring weapons. Leave the attitude.'

She didn't wait for a reply. She didn't need to. She turned and walked off like she'd just handed down a royal decree and expected it to be obeyed.

The tavern didn't go back to normal. Not right away. Conversations resumed, yes, but softer. Warier. Every drink tasted slightly stronger; every laugh came with a nervous glance towards the door she'd vanished through.

As she passed a table of sellswords, one of them started to rise: just a twitch, a movement of interest or foolish bravado, but he caught her glance and thought better of it. He sat back down without a word, suddenly fascinated by the foam on his ale.

Kril muttered under his breath, 'She's already decided, hasn't she?'

Adanion sipped the rum, finally. 'Oh, she already did. She just hasn't admitted it yet.'

He turned the glass thoughtfully in his fingers, watching the amber liquid swirl. The rim still held the faint impression of her mouth, and for a heartbeat, he considered stealing the glass as a souvenir. But no, too dramatic, even for him.

Kril sighed. 'You're going to flirt with her the whole way, aren't you?'

'I'm going to work with her,' Adanion replied. 'Professionally. Respectfully. Sensually.'

'This is going to end in blood.'

'Most good things do. I consider it motivation.'

Kril grunted. 'She's going to murder you.'

'I'd die smiling.'

And that, more than anything, was what Kril found most concerning. Adanion meant it. He always did.

The elf wasn't reckless, not exactly. But he had a way of chasing danger like it owed him something. Maybe it did. Maybe it was something he was trying to outrun: some noble scandal, some forgotten war, some ghost with his name carved into its bones. Kril had long since stopped asking. Some stories were better left buried.

Still, he didn't like the look in Adanion's eyes just now. That flicker of fascination. Not lust, though that was always there. No—this was worse: Curiosity. That bone-deep itch that pulled him into vaults, pits, and trouble. That hunger for answers to questions no sane man would ask.

They stood in silence a moment, watching the orc disappear through the door she came in. The tavern slowly resumed its noise and movement: nervous laughter, cards slapping against wood, the distant sound of someone retching in a bucket behind the bar.

'You ever just think we should look before we leap?' Adanion asked.

Kril snorted. 'We always look. We just don't stop.'

Adanion nodded. 'Fair enough.'

Somewhere near the hearth, the bard picked up his tune again. He'd shifted from a ballad to something darker now, something with minor chords and a beat that sounded a bit too much like footsteps in a tunnel.

Kril scratched his chin. 'We still have half a barrel of mead.'

Adanion didn't answer right away. His eyes were still on the door, lips parted slightly in a grin that was equal parts challenge and delight. Not at the danger. Not even at the coin. At her. That walk, that voice, that iron certainty.

'We also have a vault job, a midnight rendezvous, and a woman who could kill you with a wink.'

Kril rolled his eyes and downed the last of his mead in one long swallow, setting the mug aside with a thud. 'I liked it better when we hunted goblins.'

'You were mauled by a dire goat.'

'Not my fault. And still easier than flirting.'

Adanion didn't argue. He crossed to the dark corner near the stairs where his pack rested, pulling out a fitted tunic of thick, dark leather, reinforced subtly at the shoulders and chest.

He shed the wine-stained linen shirt he was wearing, tossing it carelessly towards the barmaid's station. 'One down,' he murmured.

Kril shook his head. 'That was a perfectly good shirt.'

Adanion pulled the leather on with a smooth flex of his shoulders, the new material catching the firelight. 'A gentleman must manage his wardrobe. Can't go to a job interview smelling of stale ale and good times, now can I?'

He then retrieved his rapier from the coat hook: silver-chased and elegant, with a grip wrapped in midnight blue. He drew it slightly from the scabbard and gave it a testing flick. The blade hummed softly as it settled. Still perfectly balanced. Still impossibly sharp. 'You name yours yet?' Kril asked.

'My sword? No,' Adanion said, sliding it home. 'I don't name things I sleep with.'

Kril snorted. 'Wouldn't that make it more likely, in your

case?'

Adanion's grin widened. 'Tempting. But I find mystery adds to the thrill.'

They stepped away from their table, the sounds of the tavern dimming behind them. The floorboards creaked under Kril's weight as they made for the door, their footsteps oddly synchronised. Outside, the rain had lessened to a fine drizzle, but the streets still glistened with puddles and half-lit reflections.

A gust of cold wind swept in as Adanion pulled open the tavern door. The fire behind them flickered violently in protest, sending shadows dancing across the walls like startled spirits. Kril ducked his head slightly to avoid the frame and stepped out into the night.

The village looked no more welcoming than it had on arrival. The crooked houses leaned like drunkards huddling against the wind. Lanterns swung on rusted chains, casting jittery pools of orange across the cobbles. Somewhere in the distance, a dog barked. Or something that sounded enough like a dog to worry Kril.

'You think she'll show?' Kril asked, adjusting the strap on his shoulder.

'She said midnight,' Adanion replied, his eyes scanning the low hills beyond the village. 'Orcish honour. She'll be there.'

'You really think it's honour keeping her honest?'

Adanion smiled. 'No. I think it's confidence. She expects us to follow. So we will.'

Kril gave him a sidelong look. 'And if she doesn't?'

'Then we drink the rest of that mead and pretend this conversation never happened.'

'Fair.'

They stood for a moment in silence, letting the night settle around them. The clouds parted briefly overhead, revealing a sliver of moonlight that gleamed against Kril's axe and caught in the silver strands of Adanion's hair.

The world smelled like rain and woodsmoke and something old waking up beneath the hills.

Kril adjusted his grip on his axe. 'You know this is going to end badly.'

Adanion's smile didn't fade. If anything, it grew. 'Oh, I do hope so.'

He turned back towards the tavern and caught sight of the barmaid passing with a tray of drinks. With a flick of his fingers, he tossed her a gold coin.

'Well then,' he said, 'we'd better sharpen our weapons.'

She caught the coin mid-air and flashed him a sly smile. No words, just a knowing nod, like it had always belonged in her apron.

'Sharpen yours,' Kril replied, stretching with a crack of his shoulders. 'Lorna's always ready.'

CHAPTER TWO

THE ORC, THE OFFER, AND THE IDIOT WITH THE LUTE

T HE OLD CHAPEL HAD LONG since fallen from grace.
Its once-stained glass windows were now jagged mosaics of coloured shards, cracked and weather-worn. Moonlight streamed through the gaps, casting fractured pools of red, blue, and gold across the crumbling flagstone floor. Vines crawled through what was once the western wall, their tendrils snaking towards the broken altar as if reaching for absolution.

A pair of candles wavered like hesitant breaths near the back, barely illuminating the figure seated on the cracked marble bench.

Rhazha.

They didn't know her name yet. Not officially. Adanion had a hunch, drawn from a few whispered descriptions and the vague trail of broken noses she left behind, but he hadn't asked. Not yet.

She sat with one leg folded over the other, twin axes leaning casually against the wall beside her. In her hands, she turned a dagger slowly, methodically sharpening its already gleaming edge with a whetstone. The sound was soft, rhythmic, patient. Dangerous.

Above her, wind whispered through the rafters where the ceiling had given way. Each gust stirred the ivy along the walls, making the chapel feel not so much abandoned as... watchful. Shadows flickered across the walls, cast by the movement of dying leaves and the flickering candles.

A faint heat seemed to simmer beneath the cold stones, like a whispered warning just beneath the surface.

Rhazha didn't flinch. She sat as though carved from the same stone that lined the ruined floor, as though she had all the time in the world—and none to waste.

Shadows flickered, restless, as if the very air held a secret waiting to be claimed.

The altar, now little more than a broken slab, had once held relics. Dust coated its surface, interrupted only by the imprint of something large and rectangular that had been recently removed. Or stolen.

The stone where it had once rested was blackened, not with soot but with something deeper, as though the altar itself had recoiled from its touch. Even in absence, the space seemed to hum faintly, a silence too deliberate to be natural.

No offerings remained. No symbols. Just silence and the scent of wet moss, old wax, and colder things.

She paused her sharpening, tilting her head slightly as if listening. A soft creak. The crunch of boots on broken tile.

And then—

Adanion emerged from the shadowed doorway, his cloak fluttering behind him like the beginning of a better story. He stepped lightly over the ruined stone and broken pews, each footfall echoing just slightly more than he would have liked.

His silver hair caught the moonlight, of course. It always did.

Kril followed a few steps behind, ducking slightly to avoid what remained of the arched doorway. The half-giant looked entirely out of place in the delicate ruin. Too solid. Too alive. He carried the weight of the chapel's collapse in each step—and looked mildly annoyed about it.

'This doesn't scream "safe job offer",' Kril muttered, his voice a low rumble that barely stirred the still air.

'No,' Adanion agreed, smiling faintly, 'but it does whisper 'mystery and opportunity,' and you know how I get around whispers.'

The chapel wasn't entirely abandoned. Someone had been using it as a hiding place—thin bedroll in one corner, a few crumbs, the faint reek of cheap ale. His name, as it turned out, was Fenwick, and he hadn't chosen the ruin for its charm. He'd been here long before Adanion and Kril arrived, hiding from a tavern he could no longer drink in and, more importantly, from a butcher's husband who'd taken offence at his latest ballad. The chapel promised obscurity and 'perfect acoustics' for a masterpiece only he believed in. What it delivered was a front-row seat to Adanion and Kril's arrival—and the kind of trouble Fenwick claimed to hate but could never resist.

From somewhere near the shattered organ pipes came a thin, out-of-tune melody. The notes wobbled and clanged, but there was a certain infectious enthusiasm behind the effort.

A skinny bard with a mop of tangled hair sat cross-legged on a pile of broken pews, the lute was nearly bigger than him. His fingers danced over the strings with more enthusiasm than skill. The strings buzzed and twanged, filling the ruined chapel with off-key music that somehow lifted the tension.

Kril narrowed his eyes at the bard, squinting like one

might a recurring rash. 'The infamous Fenwick, isn't it? Still alive, still making noise. I should've guessed.'

'"Fenwick... isn't it?"' Fenwick replied. 'YOU KNOW DAMN WELL WHO I AM, you goat-herding golem!'

Fenwick scoffed. 'And infamous? Please. I'm a *legend*. Just underappreciated by giants and the tone-deaf.'

Kril muttered, 'Confusion, nausea—same result. And you got me mauled by a dire goat.'

'That was a bloody accident, and I apologised for months!'

Adanion grinned. 'Every time with you two.'

Fenwick slung the lute forward with a flourish. 'Anyway, one verse of The Ballad of Fenwick the Daring—guaranteed to stir hearts, moisten eyes, and possibly loosen trousers.'

'Please don't,' Kril replied.

He struck a grand chord. A string snapped.

Kril didn't blink. 'Stirred something, all right. Think it was my breakfast.'

Fenwick paused. Then strummed a pitiful two-string chord.

'It's um... a minimalist arrangement now.'

Adanion covered a grin. 'Bold artistic choice.'

Fenwick huffed, brushing dust from his sleeve as though the whole tumble had been deliberate. 'Anyway, it's quieter here than the tavern. Fewer drunks throwing bottles. Fewer husbands chasing me with cleavers.'

Adanion raised an eyebrow, green eyes glinting. 'Fewer, perhaps. None? Questionable.'

Fenwick caught Adanion's eye and gave a hopeful thumbs-up. Then, with a flourish clearly meant to impress, he stood—forgot the lute strap tangled round his boot—and toppled backwards off the pews with a yelp.

The lute gave a sorrowful twang. Dust rose like applause.

Rhazha didn't look impressed. 'You brought a walking disaster zone.'

'Ah,' Adanion said, sweeping his cloak aside with theatrical flair, 'but every disaster needs a soundtrack.'

Rhazha eyed him with a mix of amusement and caution, then her gaze slid to Kril. 'And your pet boulder made it, too. I'm shocked.'

Kril grunted and crossed his arms. The chapel creaked somewhere overhead, as if offering its own warning.

'So let me get this straight,' Adanion said, stepping closer and swirling a silver flask instead of his usual wine glass. He hadn't trusted the tavern's goblets since the Rat Incident. 'You need two skilled fighters to retrieve an artefact from the Bonecrack Ruins. It's guarded, cursed, and possibly haunted. And the reward is...?'

The woman finally leaned forward into the light, her Orcish features cast in gold and shadow.

'Enough gold to swim in. If you don't mind bleeding a little first.'

'I bleed beautifully,' Adanion said, flashing teeth.

'Don't encourage him,' Kril rumbled, eyeing a spider crawling across the altar. He squashed it with one calloused thumb.

She ignored the comment. 'You ever dealt with hex-bound vaults?'

'I've flirted with two cursed priestesses, three necromancers, and a banshee named Laurel who tried to drown me with a kiss. Twice.' Adanion offered. 'How different can it be?'

She raised a brow. 'You lived through all that?'

Kril spoke up: 'He flirted. I did the living-through.'

She smirked. 'Then maybe I hired the right pair.'

Adanion stepped closer, and for a moment, the usual

lightness in his posture faded. His voice lowered just a note. 'Why the Bonecrack Ruins? What's so special that you—of all people—are hiring outsiders for a smash-and-grab?'

There was a pause. The candle between them hissed.

The orc woman set the dagger down, the metal clinking on the stone beside her.

'Because the ruins sit on cursed ground. The kind that likes to play tricks with the mind. Makes men forget their names. Makes strong warriors turn on their allies. I need people immune to that kind of nonsense.'

'You think we qualify?' Adanion asked.

'You're stupid enough to chase a job on rumour alone, charming enough to lie through your teeth, and stubborn enough to keep coming even when it's clearly a trap.' She stood. 'Yes. I think you qualify.'

Kril scowled. 'Did she just compliment us or insult us?'

'Both,' Adanion said, grinning.

She reached for one of her axes, slinging it across her back. Then, almost as an afterthought—

'My name's Rhazha,' she said. 'Remember it.'

Then she stepped forward, close enough that Adanion caught the sharp scent of leather and cold steel mingling with the faint trace of earth and smoke on her skin. The flickering candlelight caught in her eyes, setting them ablaze with a fierce golden glow. They weren't eyes that invited trust—not yet—but they promised danger and certainty.

'Meet me at dawn,' she said, voice low and gravelled, carrying the weight of command. 'One league north of town. Bring weapons. Bring silence. And don't make me regret this.'

She brushed past Adanion without hesitation, her presence slipping past him like a shadow—close enough to brush shoulders, then gone.

Kril remained where he was, watching the doorway as

she paused and turned. Her gaze locked on him, sharp and amused in the dim light.

'And you?' she said, voice dropping to a teasing growl. 'Try not to squash any more wildlife. The gods here are twitchy.'

Kril looked down, following her gaze to the crushed spider flattened beneath his boot. He shrugged, a crooked grin tugging at his lips. 'It started it.'

Rhazha's lips quirked, just for a moment, before she slipped through the broken doorway like she'd never been there at all, swallowed up by the shadows and the chill night beyond.

The chapel door swung closed with a reluctant groan, sealing the trio inside the shadows and dust.

Fenwick's lute hummed again, uncertain but eager, as if sensing the weight pressing down on the room. Adanion gave the instrument a sidelong glance, lips twitching. 'You sure that thing isn't cursed?'

Fenwick shrugged, plucking a string that buzzed slightly out of tune. 'Only on Tuesdays.' His grin was as thin and sharp as a blade's edge, but his eyes flicked nervously towards the dark corners where the moonlight failed to reach.

Kril scuffed a boot against a loose tile, eyes narrowing on the broken altar. 'So, what exactly are we walking into at dawn? Ghosts? Bandits? Angry spirits?' His voice was low, steady—enough to mask the unease crawling beneath.

Adanion's smile tightened. 'Something tells me Rhazha's not inviting us to tea and polite conversation.'

'Pretty sure she's the kind who kills first and asks questions later,' Kril added, glancing towards the shattered window where the cold night seeped in, carrying the faint scent of damp earth and rusted iron.

A silence fell, heavy and watchful, as if the very stones were holding their breath. Outside, the wind threaded through the broken rafters, stirring the ivy and carrying faint scents—wet moss, cold earth, and something metallic, sharp and unspoken.

Fenwick strummed a hesitant chord, the notes weaving through the tension like a fragile thread. 'I say we rest up. The night is still young, and dawn comes cruel.'

Adanion nodded. 'Agreed. We'll need every edge when we meet her.'

Kril kicked at a loose stone, sending it skittering across the floor. 'Yeah, and if it's anything like her, we'll be lucky to leave in one piece.'

A faint scrape echoed from the back of the chapel. All three froze, breaths caught. Kril's hand twitched towards his dagger. But it was only a rat, quick and shadowed, darting between fallen pews and splintered beams.

Adanion let out a breath, chuckling softly. 'See? Just the wildlife.'

Kril gave the spider's crushed remains a final glare before shaking his head. 'Wildlife that wants us dead, maybe.'

The candles sputtered low, flickering with fragile breaths as the chill seeped deeper into the stones. Fenwick strummed again, this time with a little more confidence, weaving a tune equal parts warning and charm, its notes curling in the damp air like smoke.

Adanion stepped towards the shattered altar, fingers tracing the dust-covered imprint of the missing relic. 'Whatever was here…' His voice trailed off. 'Someone's been looking for it. Or something.'

Kril joined him, eyes scanning the worn carvings at the altar's edge. 'Doesn't look like a simple theft. More like… a message.'

A long silence stretched, the kind that presses heavy in the lungs. Outside, the village slept beneath a cold moon, unaware of the shadows stirring just beyond its borders.

Adanion turned to his companions, eyes sharp and sure. 'We rest now, but at first light, we find Rhazha. And we find out what she's guarding—and why.'

Kril grunted in agreement. 'I'm not thrilled, but I'm in.'

Fenwick nodded, fingers poised over the lute strings. 'Then let's hope the music keeps us alive.'

Kril rolled his eyes. 'Dani, you realise she might kill us, right?'

Adanion adjusted his cloak, a slow smile curving his lips. 'I think she likes me.'

Kril snorted, crossing his arms. 'You're definitely going to get us killed.'

Adanion's smile didn't fade. 'Maybe. But it'll be both worth it and entertaining.'

The faint buzz of Fenwick's lute filled the quiet space, uncertain notes trembling in the candlelight. The chapel seemed to settle around them, ancient stones shifting and sighing as if alive. Outside, the wind slipped in through broken panes and cracked rafters, carrying secrets wrapped in cold moonlight.

The three stood in a hushed stillness, the echoes of Rhazha's footsteps fading into the night beyond the shattered door.

Kril gave the chapel one last suspicious glance, voice low and tense. 'I don't like this place. The air feels heavy—like there's something in it, watching us.'

Adanion smirked, clasping his hands behind his back and tilting his head with easy confidence. 'That's the curse talking. Or your imagination. Probably both.'

Fenwick plucked a hesitant note from his lute, a nervous

grin spreading across his face. 'You think curses are just stories, yeah? Like songs made up to scare children.'

Adanion turned and regarded the bard thoughtfully. 'And what's your speciality, Fenwick? Besides scaring away any decent musicians?'

'I write songs about fools who do stupid things and live to tell the tale,' Fenwick said, strumming a deliberate chord. 'Mostly fools who make friends with orcs and elves and giants, and go hunting ghosts in cursed ruins.'

Kril laughed, shaking his head. 'Sounds like my kind of story.'

They shared a brief laugh before the conversation faded under the weight of what lay ahead.

Adanion paced the chapel floor, the silence stretching long enough to make the stones beneath feel alive. The candles flared once, then dimmed, their flames bending like bowing reeds as a draft teased secrets through the ruined chapel. The cracked flagstones felt cold beneath his boots. The scent of damp earth and old stone wrapped the room like a shroud.

He pulled his cloak tighter. 'Alright, you two,' he chuckled, shaking his head. 'We meet at dawn. Come morning, we'll see who's still standing. Until then, rest well, idiots.'

Fenwick looked thoughtful. 'So, what's the plan? Just walk in, grab the shiny thing, and run like hell?'

Adanion smiled a crooked grin. 'I'd wager it's not going to be that simple.'

The chapel settled around them, groaning softly overhead with a low, mournful creak as a breeze stirred the tattered curtains hanging in broken windows. Outside, the moon dipped behind ragged clouds, and the night deepened, thick with promise and danger.

CHAPTER THREE

PACKING, PACING, AND A PROBLEM WITH MAPS

By the time dawn broke, Kril was already regretting everything.

It had rained in the night—just enough to soak the saddle, dampen his boots, and make everything smell like wet goat and mildew. His mood matched the sky: grey, surly, and threatening to crack open with thunder at any moment.

The horses they'd borrowed were moody and smelled worse than the tavern. Their hooves clopped unevenly on the rough cobblestones, and they tossed their heads, as if promising mischief before the journey had barely begun.

The mare Kril had drawn seemed to resent him, on a spiritual level. She kept jerking the reins and snorting like he'd insulted her ancestry. Which, knowing Kril, he probably had.

Adanion, true to form, had packed only a single satchel—mostly full of hair oil, wine, and a silver brush adorned with a moon-shaped sigil.

'Do you ever pack weapons?' Kril grunted, eyeing Adanion's bag with suspicion.

Adanion tapped the hilt of the thin Aevrinai blade at his hip with a lazy finger. 'I bring what I need.'

'You brought three shirts,' Kril pointed out, blinking at the soft folds of fabric peeking out of the satchel.

'They breathe well,' Adanion replied smoothly, adjusting his silver hair as if that settled the matter.

Kril grumbled and adjusted the heavy pack on his back. It contained food, rope, a spare axe, bedrolls, and basically everything useful. He was starting to think 'best friend' was Aevreneth for 'walking storage unit.'

As they reached the edge of the Hollow, Kril glanced back once—just long enough to see the crooked roofline of the tavern where it had all started, sagging under the weight of its own bad decisions and worse ale. Smoke trickled from its chimney like a lazy farewell. He sighed. It was too late to back out now. Besides, someone had to make sure Adanion didn't get himself eaten by accident.

The morning air was crisp but carried the faint tang of damp earth and woodsmoke from chimneys still burning in Deadgoat Hollow. A few stragglers wandered past the tavern, casting curious glances at the three figures preparing for departure.

They found Rhazha waiting by a crooked stone marker in the shadow of an old twisted tree, its bark blackened by lightning and time. Her horse was larger than both of theirs combined, jet black and armour-plated, its breath steaming in the cool air like a living shadow.

She looked like a statue carved from war itself—still, powerful, and not particularly patient.

'You're late.' Without looking up, she ran a callused hand over the pommel of one of the axes strapped to her back.

'We're fashionably late,' Adanion replied with a grin, sliding his satchel over his shoulder. 'There's a difference.'

Rhazha's eyes flicked to the satchel as she tossed him a map, its edges worn and creased. He fumbled it, the parchment slipping from his fingers until Kril caught it with two careful fingers.

'The crystals are here,' she said, her voice dropping. 'The heart-shaped one hums with a strange warmth. The other, the dark one... it feels like a wound.'

'Bonecrack Ruins are two days east, past goblin territory. If we're lucky, we only have to kill a few dozen.'

'If we're lucky?' Kril echoed, tone flat.

Adanion smiled, glancing at Kril with mock optimism. 'Think of it as cardio.'

Fenwick, the bard whose off-key lute had been the evening's unwelcome soundtrack, shuffled up beside them, clutching his battered instrument like a life raft.

'I'll see you lot off,' Fenwick said, voice hopeful but hesitant.

Kril raised an eyebrow. 'Brave of you—to the gate and no farther. See us off, then see yourself somewhere safe.'

Fenwick swallowed. 'Nah, I'm good. I heard there's a tavern in Mudwater that I want to check out. Said they wanted live music, and I'm pretty sure it's a place that's a bit less... deadly.'

Adanion smirked. 'Wise choice. I'd hate to have to lug your sorry arse out of a trap.'

Fenwick grinned, the tension breaking like a shattered lute string. 'I'll keep the tavern alive in your honour. Mayhaps write a song or two—if it's safe.'

He gave them a quick salute and turned, his footsteps fading on the cobblestones as the sun climbed higher.

Adanion watched him go. 'Good riddance.'

Kril snorted. 'No more singing.'

Rhazha rolled her eyes but smiled slightly. 'Thank the

gods.'

They saddled up, the horses' metal hooves ringing against stone as they moved out of the Hollow and into the tangled forests beyond.

They rode in silence for a time. Birds called overhead, their songs sharp and fleeting. The wind whistled through trees twisted like claws, their branches clawing at the sky as if to snatch at passing clouds.

The path east wasn't much of a path at all—more a series of deer tracks that wound between leaning trees and mossy stumps. Brambles clawed at their boots. Mud sucked at the horses' hooves. A few times, Kril had to dismount and clear fallen branches or check for hidden dips in the forest floor where water pooled, dark and stagnant.

Adanion hummed now and then, mostly to himself. Occasionally, he offered commentary on the foliage.

'Tragic, really. If these trees had better lighting and a competent gardener, they could be spectacular,' he noted.

Kril ignored him. Rhazha didn't.

'Do you ever shut up?' she asked at one point, brushing a low-hanging branch aside with her axe haft.

Adanion tilted his head thoughtfully. 'Not if I can avoid it.'

Rhazha muttered something in Orhzaan that sounded deeply uncomplimentary.

She was a quiet rider, all sharp eyes and soft footfalls, which made Kril like her immediately. She didn't fill the silence unless there was something worth saying. She didn't ask about their quest, their past, or their reasons. She rode like she knew the forest and didn't trust it—and the forest returned the sentiment.

A flock of crows burst out of the treetops as they passed beneath an old archway of stone, swallowed by vines. The birds cried out like old ghosts, wheeling overhead before vanishing into the grey sky.

Rhazha finally broke the silence. 'So. You two work together long?'

Kril snorted. 'Since Adanion accidentally seduced a baron's daughter.'

'She was very persuasive,' Adanion defended, his grin turning cocky. 'And I didn't know she was married.'

'You did,' Kril corrected, voice low. 'You just didn't care.'

'I still don't.'

Rhazha laughed—a low, dangerous sound that rode the wind like a promise or a threat. 'I like you two.'

Kril looked at Adanion and shook his head. 'See? First sign of madness.'

By midday, the forest began to thin, giving way to broad hills dotted with standing stones and cairns. A trail of ancient markers guided them like bone-white teeth jutting from the soil. Rhazha dismounted at one point to examine a cracked monolith.

'This one's been defaced,' she murmured, brushing moss away to reveal a gouged symbol. 'Gnoll markings.'

'Friendly?' Adanion asked, from a safe distance.

'No, she said. 'Hungry.'

They pressed on. The map was detailed but difficult to read in the flickering light of campfires and starlit nights. Every night, Rhazha studied the parchment carefully, tracing routes with a callused finger and pointing out dangers hidden beneath layers of moss and stone.

She muttered to herself while she worked—names of old roads, warnings in broken dialects, words like 'bloodstone' and 'sinkhole' and 'no return.'

One evening, as the fire crackled between them, Kril caught Adanion examining the map upside down. 'You're holding it wrong,' he said drily.

Adanion squinted. 'It's a map, not a magic mirror. It works either way.'

Rhazha snorted. 'You might be the worst navigator I've ever seen.'

Adanion shrugged. 'I'm better with directions than most, but maps? That's a whole different beast.'

Kril chuckled. 'She's right. You couldn't find your way out of a broom closet.'

They took turns on watch, rotating through shifts with the tired resignation of people who knew sleep was a luxury. Kril's shifts were quiet, save for the creak of trees and the crackle of flames. Once, he thought he heard something breathing just beyond the firelight. Something large. But when he rose and turned, there was only the empty dark, thick and silent as a closed tomb.

The banter eased the tension, but as the days wore on, the weight of what lay ahead grew heavier.

At one point, they found themselves standing at the edge of a sheer cliff, the ruins far below—a jagged scar against the forest floor.

The descent had come sooner than expected. One moment, the trees parted, and the next, the land simply stopped. Beyond the edge lay a chasm, carved long ago by wind or magic—or both. The artefact waited somewhere deep beneath the stone and ruin, its presence felt more than seen.

'That's the place,' Rhazha said, voice low.

They dismounted. The horses pawed nervously at the ground, their ears flicking back and forth. Kril ran a hand down his mount's neck to calm it, though his own stomach twisted with unease.

Adanion surveyed the drop, calculating. 'Looks easy to get down. The hard part will be getting back up.'

'Don't get cocky,' Rhazha warned.

He gave her a sly smile. 'I'm always cocky. It's part of my charm.'

She didn't laugh, which Kril silently appreciated.

The descent was slow and treacherous. Roots jutted from the cliffside like the bones of buried giants. Loose stones skittered beneath their boots. Rhazha led, finding paths that looked impossible until they weren't. Kril followed, eyes on the ground, axe strapped tightly across his back.

Adanion came last, muttering complaints under his breath about chipped nails and uncooperative boots.

The temperature dropped as they moved downward, the air thickening like soup left too long in a cauldron. Mist coiled along the ground, veiling the jagged stones and warped architecture of the ruins. Massive blocks lay scattered like the bones of gods. Half-toppled arches leaned against one another, held aloft by centuries of defiance and rot. The air grew colder and thicker, as if the stones themselves breathed unease, and the deeper they went, the more the shadows pressed in.

Rhazha paused. 'This is where the traps start.'

She knelt and ran a hand over the mossy ground. Her fingers brushed against something—a thin, barely visible groove. She nodded to herself and took three steps to the right before motioning them forward.

Kril tightened his grip on his axe, eyes scanning shadows.

Adanion flicked a glance to the map, trying to reconcile the worn symbols with what lay before them. 'I think this was a courtyard once,' he murmured, gesturing at the stone slabs and shattered pillars.

'Now it's a kill zone,' Rhazha replied, voice flat.

Suddenly, a faint click echoed beneath their feet.

'Trap,' Rhazha hissed, leaping back as a net shot up from the ground, barely missing Kril's leg.

He yanked free and brought his axe down in a single, brutal swing, severing the net's anchor with a spray of dirt and snapped rope.

And then the ruin exploded with motion.

Figures burst from the crumbled stone—dozens of goblins, their shrieks high and maddening, echoing off the moss-slick walls. They came crawling from broken archways, dropping from ledges, skittering across rubble with blades in their jagged little fists and murder in their eyes.

Kril didn't think. He moved.

The first goblin lunged. His axe caught it mid-leap, splitting it from collarbone to hip. Another surged in behind, jabbing with a crooked spear. Kril twisted, the point grazing his shoulder, and answered with a backhand strike that shattered its skull like overripe fruit.

To his right, Rhazha was a blur of black steel. Her axes spun, one high, one low, carving a bloody dance through the swarm. She pivoted, drove an elbow into a goblin's throat, and gutted its partner before either hit the ground. Blood sprayed across her cloak, but she didn't slow.

They kept coming. From the smoke, from the ruin, from the very earth. Small and fast—but not clever.

Adanion moved like a duellist at a masquerade, elegant and precise. He parried a flurry of strikes with a silver flourish, then slid his blade between a goblin's ribs without breaking stride. Another attacked from behind—he ducked beneath the swing and stabbed upward, his blade sliding beneath the creature's chin, snapping its head back with a wet crunch.

'They're coordinated!' Kril shouted, swinging in a brutal arc that sent three goblins tumbling like kindling. 'Since when do goblins plan ambushes?'

'The clever ones,' Rhazha growled, ripping her axe free from a chest cavity. 'We're not dealing with a random pack—this was set!'

'Brilliant,' Adanion muttered, sidestepping a hurled dagger and returning the favour with one of his own. It struck its mark with surgical precision—right through the eye.

For every goblin that fell, two more clambered forward over their bodies. The air reeked of blood, sweat, and smoke. Kril felt the thrum in his bones—that battle-pulse that drowned out fear and thought and made everything feel sharp. Every move mattered. Every mistake could end him.

He locked eyes with Rhazha across the chaos—just for a heartbeat—and they moved. Together.

She leapt from a toppled column, landing beside him just as two goblins broke through the melee. Kril slammed one aside with his shield, and Rhazha took the other's legs out from under it before finishing the job with a downward strike that cracked stone.

Adanion, above them now—somehow above—had scaled the ruin wall and launched himself into a diving spin, his cloak flaring behind him like a shadowy wing. He landed atop a goblin captain, driving his blade through the creature's collar and into the ground. The others hesitated—just for a moment. It was enough.

Kril roared and charged, a bull in armour, his axe carving wide arcs. Goblins scattered or fell. He smashed through a tangle of rusted spears, caught one attacker mid-lunge and threw him into a pillar, bone snapping like firewood.

Finally—mercifully—the swarm broke. A few survivors squealed and vanished into the ruins' dark edges.

When silence fell, the ruin was still, save for the ragged breaths of the three warriors.

'Only a dozen more of those and we'll be broke,' Kril muttered.

'Or dead,' Adanion added.

The silence that followed didn't feel like peace—it felt emptied. The kind of quiet that only came after violence, thick and heavy, as though the ruins themselves were waiting to see if anyone else dared move.

Kril leaned on his axe, breath heaving. Blood—most of it not his—dripped from the blade in slow, sticky trails. One glob hit the stone with a soft splatter. He looked around, wary for another wave, but the rubble-strewn courtyard had stilled.

Adanion ran a hand through his hair, flicking goblin gore off his cheek with a grimace. 'Disgusting creatures. No sense of hygiene, tactics, or drama.'

Rhazha said nothing. She crouched beside a fallen goblin captain, its rusted helm split open by her axe. With the toe of her boot, she turned the body and studied the markings on its leathers—tiny sigils carved into the straps, burn marks around the edges. Not random. Not common.

Her brows drew together.

'Black Fang,' she muttered, half to herself. 'Clever, methodical. They don't just strike—they follow patterns. I know how they think.' Offshoot of the Iron Tusks. Used to raid border villages. They don't usually come this far west.'

Adanion raised an eyebrow. 'I don't like 'usually.' Especially when it's being rewritten in real time.'

'They were absorbed. Or so we thought.' Her voice dropped, low and steady. 'And if they took something, it wouldn't be random. They have a system—hiding things where they know they can find them later. They don't just raid; they follow a method. A ritual, almost. Always taking the most valuable parts first. But this... this wasn't some aimless fight. They knew exactly what they were doing. Like they were following orders.'

Kril scanned the dead, jaw tight. 'Orders?' He wiped his brow with a grimy cloth, then tossed it aside. 'From who? Some goblin warlord with a clipboard?' He kicked at a crumpled body. 'Does this mean someone sent them?'

Rhazha nodded once. 'We can figure out their habits if we need to, and who—or what—drove them here.'

That thought settled over them like a fog.

For a moment, no one spoke.

Only the wind stirred through the broken stones, carrying the scent of blood, rust, and moss. Far above, the forest canopy whispered as if in mourning. Even the goblins' bodies seemed to lie too still, as though the violence had pulled the life out of the world itself.

Rhazha rose slowly, wiping her axe clean on the captain's cloak. The blade caught the firelight with a dull glint, its edge nicked but still sharp. She didn't speak—just nodded once, and that was enough.

Kril shifted his weight with a grunt. His shoulders ached from the weight of his swings, and his left knee throbbed where a goblin had caught him off balance with a jagged blade. He adjusted the grip on his axe and scanned the darkness ahead, but his gaze kept drifting back to the fallen. Not guilt—just awareness. The kind you don't lose once it's earned.

Adanion moved last. He sheathed his sword with a theatrical flick, then brushed dirt from his coat like he'd just stepped out of a garden party. His eyes, though, lingered a heartbeat too long on the nearest goblin corpse before he smiled.

'Well,' he said, breaking the heaviness with a familiar smirk, 'I suppose that qualifies as our morning exercise. Shall we risk death some more?'

Kril didn't smile, but something in his shoulders eased. The banter was good. Banter meant normal. Banter meant they were still alive.

Rhazha didn't answer immediately. She checked the bindings on her gauntlets, fingers moving in smooth, practised motions. Then she glanced at the others.

'Stay sharp,' she said, voice low. 'We're not through yet.'

They moved slowly now, steps deliberate and quiet. The labyrinth seemed to close in tighter the deeper they went—stone corridors narrowing, the walls damp and cold to the touch, covered in moss that curled like old parchment. Somewhere ahead, water dripped rhythmically, echoing in the silence like a distant clock counting down.

They passed carvings etched into the walls—symbols older than any of them could name. Some were defaced, others still glowing faintly with dying magic. Whatever power had once ruled these ruins, it hadn't left quietly.

They pressed deeper into the labyrinth, guided by Rhazha's careful knowledge and their shared will to survive.

Whatever warded the place had held for centuries—but the spell was thinning now, strained over something still humming with power.

And they would need every ounce of strength, every shred of cunning, to claim it.

They emerged from the ruin's shadows just as the forest began to wake—mist curling low, and something unseen watching from the trees.

Kril took one look at the looming treeline and muttered, 'This place better not have spiders.'

CHAPTER FOUR

GOBLINS ARE TERRIBLE AT AMBUSHES

THE AIR SHIFTED, THICKER NOW—HUMID, unmoving, almost cloying. This was Everdark Forest, where branches twisted above like claws, blotting out what little sky remained. Every step forward felt like stepping further from the world they knew, and deeper into one that had been forgotten on purpose.

Kril's hand drifted to his axe more than once, fingers flexing. Not fear. Not quite. But something had set his instincts to a slow, cold crawl.

'Still no birds,' he muttered.

'No squirrels either,' Rhazha replied, voice low. 'Forest this dense should be crawling with them.'

Adanion lifted a hand to brush away a curtain of hanging moss. 'Perhaps they've all signed up with the goblins. Unionised woodland creatures. Terrifying prospect.'

Kril snorted once, quiet and reluctant. 'You'd be the union rep. And get all the squirrels killed.'

They pressed on. The path—if it could still be called that—wound deeper into gnarled underbrush and crumbling stone. Every few paces, Rhazha paused to mark their course: a carved scratch on a root here, a strip of cloth tied to a branch there. She didn't explain, and neither of the others asked.

Mist clung to the underbrush like it had nowhere else to be, curling low and slow around tree trunks with the lazy menace of a cat watching mice. It wrapped tendrils around twisted roots and slipped through thick ferns, softening the sounds of distant movement to a near whisper. The forest smelled of wet pine needles, damp earth, and—just faintly— blood. Or maybe that was just Kril's socks again. A faint iron tang teased the nostrils, subtle but unmistakable, a warning whispered by the trees themselves. Somewhere close, an owl blinked and watched with unblinking eyes, hidden high in the branches.

Adanion strode ahead with his usual grace, the kind of Elven poise that looked like he was walking to an opera even when he was knee-deep in mud. His silver hair shimmered in stray beams, annoyingly perfect, catching glimmers of light. His long fingers rested lightly on the hilt of his sword, which gleamed as if it, too, had a personal stylist—an elegant contrast to the wildness around them.

Behind him, Kril trudged like a siege tower on legs, branches snapping underfoot. His breath puffed in slow clouds, more steam engine than man, and his battle axe hung at his side with the lazy menace of a predator sunbathing. Every now and then, his eyes darted to the shadows, wary but steady.

Rhazha brought up the rear—silent, sharp-eyed, and already regretting her life choices. The mist swirled around her like a loyal pet. Her twin axes rode easy against her back, balanced and quiet, waiting for the chance to ruin someone's day. Her gaze flickered constantly between the trees and the ground, picking up the smallest details—a snapped twig, a crushed leaf—signs of life or death long before the others noticed.

They walked in silence—partly because the forest was unnervingly quiet, and partly because none of them had had breakfast. Kril had been promised bacon. There had been no bacon.

For a brief moment, the forest held its breath.

Then—

A scream. High-pitched, frantic, gobliny. Followed immediately by a goblin tripping over its own feet and falling face-first into a bush.

Three goblins leapt from the underbrush, snarling, weapons brandished. Adanion's blade flicked once, clean and precise, cutting one down. Rhazha's axe buried itself in another's sternum. Kril grabbed the last one by its scrawny neck and slammed it into a tree so hard bark splintered. Silence fell just as quickly as it had been broken.

Adanion sheathed his sword slowly, every movement deliberate, like he was closing a story that refused to end. His eyes flicked to the surrounding trees, scanning the shadows as if expecting another wave to spring from nowhere. The first encounter had seemed almost comical in its clumsiness, yet now it left an unsettling residue, a tension that lingered in the damp air.

'That one tried to flank me,' he said, frowning, the words low but sharp. He ran a finger along the edge of his blade, as though measuring the bite of the metal against the chaos they'd just survived. 'Goblins don't flank. Not without guidance.'

Rhazha crouched slightly, her gaze sweeping over the scattered corpses, jaw tight, every muscle coiled and ready. Blood and mud splattered the forest floor, marking the goblins' frantic attempts at attack, yet there was a rhythm to the chaos, a faint pattern hidden beneath the wild flailing. They were sloppy, yes—but deliberate too, in a way that set her nerves on edge. Something—or someone—was shaping them, teaching them to move as more than just desperate scavengers.

Adanion straightened, eyes narrowing as he surveyed the clearing. The way the goblins had moved—their feints, the almost conscious way they tried to surround him—left a bitter taste. He didn't like being caught off-guard, and he didn't like surprises.

After an hour—maybe more—the forest shifted again. The trees gave way to a low ridge, ringed with standing stones. Moss-covered. Weather-worn. One of them leaned at an impossible angle, cracked through with a line that glowed faintly red, like an ember left too long in the ash.

Kril stepped up beside it, frowning. 'What's that supposed to be?'

'Old ward,' Rhazha said, tracing the crack with her eyes. 'Broken now. Whatever was sealed here… isn't.'

Adanion gave a low whistle. 'Marvellous. I do so love a cursed landmark.'

'Don't touch it,' Rhazha warned.

He lowered his hand with exaggerated care. 'Please. I've only made that mistake twice.'

They climbed the ridge in silence. At the top, the land opened into a wide, sunken clearing—a natural amphitheatre, ringed by stone outcrops and twisted vines. Something had happened here. Recently. The grass was trampled. Scorched. Blood stained the rocks in jagged arcs.

Adanion stepped forward slowly. 'This wasn't goblins.'

'No,' Rhazha said. She pointed to the centre, where the earth had been gouged deep by claws or tools. 'They were digging. Searching.'

Kril crouched near one of the bloodstains. He touched it, rubbed it between his fingers, sniffed. 'Fresh. Day old, maybe.'

'Which means they're close,' Rhazha said.
'And whatever they were looking for…' Adanion's eyes narrowed. 'Either they found it—or they're not done digging.'

The wind picked up—just a whisper, but it carried the unmistakable scent of something wrong. Not rot. Not blood. Magic. Thick. Ancient. Angry.

Kril stood. 'This the bit where we turn back and pretend we never saw it?'
Rhazha's axe rasped free. 'No. This is the bit where we find out why they wanted us dead before we got this far.'
Adanion drew his blade, calm and smooth. 'Marvellous. I was beginning to miss the tension.'

Another ambush struck without warning. Goblins sprang from pits and shadows, snarling, weapons raised. They weren't wild this time. They moved in twos, driving Kril back with thrusts while another circled for his flank. Adanion parried, ran one through, and muttered: 'They're not just scrappers. Someone's been teaching them.'

Rhazha barked orders—'Hold your ground! Don't get greedy!'—and hacked down a goblin that tried to draw her out. When the survivors melted into the mist, the three stood breathing hard, unsettled.

'Organised goblins,' Adanion said grimly. 'This isn't random.'
Rhazha spat on the ground. 'More reason to move fast. They're trying to delay us.'

The next battle was nothing like the earlier encounters. Goblins poured from both sides of the path, shrieking, blades gleaming. This was no stumble, no accident—it was an ambush, laid with purpose and malice.

Adanion moved like water, slicing through the chaos, eyes flicking to their formations. Kril bowled through a pack, laughing like thunder, though the sound had a harder edge now. Rhazha's axes carved brutal arcs, cutting down foes one after another.

The forest seemed to shudder with their cries. Branches rattled, leaves shook loose, and every strike of steel on steel rang like a bell struck too hard. Goblins came in waves, some darting from above, dropping from trees with jagged spears, others crawling from pits dug into the earth. The air stank of sweat, rot, and the copper tang of blood.

Adanion ducked beneath a spear thrust, drove his blade up through a goblin's ribs, and twisted. Another lunged from behind; he pivoted, cloak flaring, and sent its head rolling with a silver flash. Yet even he found himself pressed back a pace, boots sliding in the churned mud. 'They fight like soldiers,' he spat, voice tight. 'And I hate soldiers.'

Kril roared as three swarmed him at once. One clung to his back like a leech, dagger stabbing down, but the half-giant simply smashed its spine against a tree, crushing the wretch flat, then tore another in half with a swing of his axe. The third stabbed into Kril's thigh; Kril only laughed, scooped the goblin up by the skull, and hurled it screaming into the underbrush hard enough to break bones.

Rhazha was everywhere at once, her twin axes rising and falling in vicious rhythm. One goblin tried to grab her arm, only to lose its hand before it realised what had happened. Another leapt for her throat—she kicked it square in the chest, then split its skull when it landed. Her braid snapped behind her like a whip as she spun, low and ruthless.

Still the goblins pressed. Still they feinted, retreated, circled. It was a rhythm, a pattern—they weren't here to win.

A MODERATE CHANCE OF SCREAMING

They were here to grind the trio down.

A horn blared, deep and guttural, somewhere in the dark. The goblins surged.

Kril roared, swinging wide and felling five in a single arc. Adanion vaulted onto a fallen trunk, cutting down from above, his voice carrying sharp commands—'Left! Behind you!'—snapping out with uncharacteristic severity. Rhazha fought shoulder-to-shoulder with Kril, her smaller frame darting in to finish what his brutal swings began. Blood slicked the ground, mud sucking at their boots as they were forced into tighter formation.

At last, the tide broke. The goblins shrieked, pulled back into the trees, and melted into the mist as if swallowed.

The clearing stank of iron and smoke. The ground was carpeted with bodies and broken weapons. The silence that followed felt heavier than the fight itself.

Kril wiped blood from his mouth, grinning despite himself. 'Maybe goblins aren't so terrible at ambushes,' he said.

'Still not subtle enough,' Adanion replied, though his smirk was tinged with something darker.

Rhazha crouched beside a corpse and peeled back a rusted shoulder plate. Crude sigils, painted in black, stared back. The same Black Fang mark she had found before, but painted on a full warband's armour now. 'We're closer now,' she muttered. 'This isn't just a patrol. It's a full warband, by the looks of it. They weren't supposed to be this far west, and they're getting desperate.'

Kril loomed behind her, brow furrowed. 'Great. I love it when old enemies show up wearing someone else's leash.'

Adanion nodded, sheathing his sword. 'We'll need to be sharper. Smarter. And ready for whatever's next.'

They pressed deeper into Everdark. The trees closed in tighter, the canopy thickening until it turned the morning light to murk. Shafts of golden sun pierced through in narrow beams, illuminating nothing but fog and dust.

They walked in silence for some time. No jests. No war songs.

Then—softly, so softly it barely registered—Kril spoke. 'Never seen goblins that angry.'

'Goblins are always angry,' Rhazha replied. 'But they don't usually die this close together.'

A pause.

'...Bit messy, innit?' Kril said.

Adanion gave a short laugh—dry, but genuine. 'You could say that.'

For a few strides, the heaviness broke.

Then they saw it.

A tree up ahead—massive, ancient, split down the centre like it had been struck by lightning. But it wasn't the tree that made them pause. It was what hung from it.

A goblin corpse, nailed to the bark with a jagged spear. Runes carved into its flesh. A warning, scrawled in blood:

TURN BACK.

Kril stared at it. 'Well. That's subtle.'

Adanion stepped forward, hand on his hilt. 'They've no idea who they're dealing with.'

Rhazha didn't move. Her eyes lingered on the runes. Old ones. Deep ones.

'They weren't just told to stop us,' she said. 'They believe in what's ahead. Enough to die for it.'

A long beat of silence.

Then Adanion turned away from the corpse and strode forward, his voice low and sure.

'Then let's make sure it was all for nothing.'

They followed him—one step, then another—into the dark beyond the tree.

The forest swallowed them whole.

CHAPTER FIVE

KRIL AND THE VERY WRONG TAVERN ROMANCE

THE VILLAGE OF MUDWATER WASN'T on any official map—which, frankly, might've been its saving grace. Squat cottages leaned like drunkards, lamplit windows stared into narrow streets smelling of damp straw and muted pre-celebration, while pigs rooted in the dirt with utter confidence, as if they owned the place.

Adanion, Kril, and Rhazha trudged through creeping twilight towards the one building that looked reliably open: The Howling Tankard. Above the door, a snarling hound dripping glowing red foam swung on a loose hinge, creaking like it was begging for a lover's coin—or a curse.

Inside, they were hit with the full tavern experience: lantern light cast trembling shadows over splintered wood floors, and the air reeked of stale ale, smoked meat, and the performance anxiety of the sole bard, stubbornly replaying the same three chords like they were gold.

Fenwick hunched near the hearth, a battered lute clutched like a lifeline. His lopsided hat slid dangerously towards one eye, and he squinted at the room, measuring its chaos like a scholar studying an unsolvable equation.

Each chord he strummed was meant to be deliberate, heroic even—but his fingers kept arguing with him, landing notes that sounded more like a cough than music. Why does it feel like I'm performing in a wind tunnel? he wondered, heart skipping with every glance towards the newcomers. Are they judging me—or laughing at me? He wanted to vanish behind the barrel, to become invisible, yet some tiny spark inside told him that maybe, just maybe, this mess of a performance could matter.

A few farmers hunched at tables, whispers and last-minute bets flickered through the room, and one mysterious figure perched on a high stool, hood drawn low over their face.

Kril hesitated at the door, boots muddy, armour scraping like an ageing cart. He didn't blend with crowds—crowds made him nervous. He shifted towards a corner where he could observe: safe, silent, and out of trouble.

No such luck.

Before he could settle into his low-profile posture, a sudden pop of the door announced another arrival. A tiny halfling woman—blonde curls bouncing like spring water—slid into the seat beside him with the energy of a keg lit on fire.

'Hello, tall and terrifying,' she said, bright as a sunbeam. 'You here to drink, fight, or flirt?'

Kril's massive frame froze. He swallowed. Blinked once. '...Yes?'

She laughed—a chiming sound that turned his internal panic into something else. 'What's your name?'

Kril opened his mouth. Closed it. His hands clenched, then loosened. Then he tried again. Finally, '...Kril.'

Her smile deepened—just a little. 'Lila.'

Then her eyes lit with delight. 'Kril. Wanna dance?'

He stared. 'I don't know how.'

The halfling stood anyway. 'You just move your feet and

hope for the best.'

Kril shuffled to his feet awkwardly, feeling more like a beached whale than a dancer, but Lila was already tugging him towards the empty space by the fire. His boots scraped the rough floor, dragging a disgruntled protest from the tavern boards.

Lila's smile softened, and she gave Kril a gentle nudge. 'Don't worry, someone else will be lining up for a dance with you soon enough.'

She winked—the kind of look that meant more than friendly encouragement—making Kril's stomach do a strange flip.

Kril's eyes widened. Caught between hope and disbelief, his voice escaped before he could stop it. 'I—uh, is that a promise? Or... a threat?'

Lila laughed, tugging him back towards the warmth of the firelight. 'Depends on how many times you step on my toes next time.'

Kril swallowed hard, wondering if he'd just made a complete fool of himself. Probably.

The halfling's laughter cut through the heavy tavern air as she stepped in time with Fenwick's still-offbeat lute. Kril tried to follow, his legs betraying him with a worrying number of misplaced steps and unintended stomps.

On the far side of the room, Fenwick wrestled with his lute as if it were a wild beast with a flair for melodrama. He leaned too far forward, then back, half-perched on the barrel, eyes darting to the adventurers like a man expecting both applause and a sudden explosion. He strummed another chord—slightly off, slightly desperate—but the corners of his mouth twitched in a way that suggested he was both enjoying it and quietly panicking.

He abruptly stopped playing the background chords, drawing in a long, shaky breath. It was a sudden silence that managed to snag the attention of every drinker.

Fenwick's voice cracked as he began a hesitant ballad:
'Hear ye, hear ye, all ye brave souls,
Beware the road where the dark wind rolls!
Ghosts that wail and shadows that creep,
Where none return from their restless sleep...'

The tavern fell into a sudden hush as the words echoed—slightly off-key but earnest. Rhazha raised a brow and exchanged a glance with Adanion.

She frowned. 'Is he... turning warnings into ditties?'

Kril, still recovering from his dance debut, muttered from his corner, 'If those ghosts are anything like his singing, they'll be begging for mercy.'

Fenwick grinned sheepishly and hopped down from his stool, making his way over to their table, lute slung behind him like an ill-fitting backpack.

'It's true!' Fenwick said, eyes bright despite the rasp in his voice. 'Strange lights, eerie noises, and worse—something's stirring in the woods just outside Mudwater.'

Adanion smirked, swirling the dregs of his ale. 'Moderate chance of screaming just jumped to damn near certain.'

'Worth noting,' Rhazha said, folding her arms. 'If the road is being watched, we aren't as hidden as we thought.'

Kril sighed, rubbing his temples. 'Great. Another nightmare on top of the last one.'

Fenwick nodded earnestly. 'I promise, this time my songs come with a side of actual useful info.'

'Last night, I was trying to get a new tune just right, and I caught something odd. The locals swear they've seen shadows moving in the trees—things that don't stay still even when the wind drops. Then there's the strange howls after midnight—like the wind itself is screaming.'

Adanion arched a brow. 'The wind screaming? Poetic, if a bit dramatic.'

Fenwick shrugged. 'Bards have to keep things interesting. But I swear, there's something unnatural happening out there.'

Rhazha narrowed her eyes. 'That kind of trouble rarely stays quiet for long.'

Kril shook his head. 'Ghost stories and curses... I'm starting to think we're just walking into one disaster after another.'

'Good thing you're big, then,' Adanion grinned. 'Can crush most of them flat.'

Fenwick clapped his hands together, breaking the tension. 'Right! So, dark omens, midnight horrors, and a road that may want travellers dead. Sound like a plan?'

Adanion gave a theatrical sigh. 'Just another quiet night in Mudwater, then.'

Rhazha rose, her hand resting briefly on her blades. 'We'll move at first light. Until then, try not to get yourselves killed or turned into ghosts by dawn.'

Fenwick grinned, lute slung back in place. 'That's the spirit! I will, of course, be singing your praises from here.'

Adanion and Kril almost simultaneously rolled their eyes. 'Of course you will,' Kril grunted, with a nonplussed look on his face.

'Quiet, Golem,' Fenwick leered.

The tavern's chatter slowly returned, blending with the creak of the floorboards and the steady thrum of Fenwick's off-key lute. Outside, the moon rose high over Mudwater, casting long shadows on the crooked cottages, and the night held its breath.

It began with a tankard flying through the air. Not the usual kind of tavern spat—no growled challenge, no spilt ale—just an airborne tankard, spinning end over end like a hurled horseshoe. It struck the back wall with a hollow clang, narrowly missing a serving girl who dropped her tray and screamed.

Three goblins burst through the front window, tumbling over each other in a shrieking, tangle-limbed heap. One wore a colander strapped to his head with twine. Another clutched a rusty ladle like a mace, and the last held what looked suspiciously like a ham hock nailed to a stick. They hit the floor hard and kept going—scattering mugs, upending chairs, and charging straight into the room as if they'd been tossed by a storm.

Someone yelled, 'Raiders!' Someone else shouted, 'Bar fight!' Neither was wrong.

Adanion was first on his feet, rising with one dagger already drawn and the ghost of a sigh on his lips. Rhazha turned in her seat just as one of the goblins lunged—only to catch it mid-air with both hands, pivot, and drive its face into the bar with a splintering crunch. It slumped. She didn't blink.

Another leapt onto the table, waving its ham weapon like a war banner. Kril looked up from his darts, mildly annoyed, and threw one—not at the goblin, but at the ceiling above it. A mug dropped from the beam and struck the creature's head with a hollow thud. It dropped the ham, tottered once, and fell backwards off the table with a belch.

Lila ducked under a chair and came up with a stool in

both hands. She swung the stool like a club, missing one goblin by inches, and obliterating a row of tankards in a crash of foam and wood.

'I just ordered that!' she shouted, grabbing the nearest full pint and hurling it at another.

Fenwick tried to run and tripped over a bench. He yelped as a goblin grabbed his ankle—only for Adanion's second dagger to whistle past and pin the goblin's ear to the floor. It shrieked, more out of insult than injury.

One goblin scampered under a table and re-emerged behind the bar, brandishing a bottle of something blue and clearly flammable. It lit the end of a bar rag and began waving it like a torch. 'FIRE! FIRE! BURN THE ALE!' it cried.

'Absolutely not,' said Rhazha, and flung a tray like a discus. The bottle shattered. The torch went out. The goblin went down.

Kril moved last, slow and deliberate, rising as another tried to climb him like a post. He grabbed its ankle and spun, hurling the creature bodily through a bench, which shattered. The goblin flopped to the floor and did not get up. Kril wiped something green from his sleeve.

A final goblin shrieked something about 'vengeance for Grolf' and charged for the exit—only to find Adanion already blocking it, blade gleaming in the torchlight, wearing the grin that usually came just before trouble.

'Two choices,' Adanion said, voice silk. 'Door or dagger?'

The goblin skidded, eyes wild, then veered sideways—straight into Lila, who dropped it with a broken stool leg. It hit the floor and stayed there.

And just like that, it was over.

The goblin—or rather, goblins—had been dispatched with varying degrees of finesse, mostly involving blunt force and one very dramatic table flip. The tavern's patrons were nursing minor scrapes and several bruised egos. One gnome was still swaying on a bar stool, blinking at a broken tankard as if it had personally betrayed him.

'I liked that tankard,' he muttered.

Kril offered a sheepish nod to the patrons as he straightened a chair that had been weaponised mid-brawl. 'Sorry about the table. And the wall. And the part where I kicked a goblin through someone's soup.'

The man whose soup it had been—an elderly fellow with a beard like a frostbitten squirrel—grunted. 'Didn't like the soup anyway.'

'Still. Sorry.'

Fenwick was checking on his lute, which had suffered a grievous blow to its dignity if not its frame. 'Well,' he said, brushing goblin guts off the fingerboard, 'at least they were terrible at ambushes.'

A few chuckles rose from the tavern, and someone shouted, 'Play a song, bard!'

He opened his mouth to oblige, but then the tavern door banged shut behind a fleeing goblin, and everyone flinched.

A long silence settled. Rhazha wiped her blade on a napkin and sat, as if it were any other evening, as if they hadn't just repelled a goblin attack with equal parts violence and improvisational furniture use.

Adanion sauntered to the bar. 'Three ales,' he said, dropping a gold coin into the stunned barkeep's hand. 'And something strong for the orc.'

Kril sat where Lila had left him, broad hands clasped over one knee, cheeks tinged the colour of dying coals. His armour squeaked as he shifted uncomfortably, but he didn't move far. Just enough to glance over at the bar, where Lila had already begun chatting with the barman as if she hadn't just upended a mountain of nerves with a single dance.

Rhazha slumped into the seat beside him and set down two mugs—one frothing with dark ale, the other a glowing green concoction that probably wasn't legal. She took a sip from the latter and grimaced like it had insulted her grandmother.

'She's going to break your heart,' Rhazha said, then handed him the ale.

Kril accepted it like a relic. 'She's really... confident.'

'That's one word for it.'

He stared into the foam. 'I stepped on her foot twice.'

Rhazha's mouth twitched. 'I noticed.'

'She didn't stop.'

'Also noticed.' She leaned back and folded her arms. 'You're not bad, you know. Just... made of the wrong material for tavern twirls.'

Kril grunted. 'I'm not made for much. Breaking things, mostly. Making people nervous.'

'She didn't look nervous.'

He glanced back at Lila. She laughed, head thrown back, curls bouncing with something close to mischief.

Rhazha caught his gaze. 'You want to keep your distance, fine. Just don't pretend it's for her sake.'

Before he could reply, Adanion appeared, theatrical as ever, sliding into the seat across from them with a mug of wine in one hand and an exaggerated sigh in his chest.

'Well,' he said, clinking his goblet against Kril's ale, 'that was alarmingly sweet. I was fully prepared to place a bet on someone losing a limb.'

They shared a moment of silence, letting Fenwick's terrible lute fill the void like a determined mosquito with delusions of grandeur.

'I think she likes me,' Kril said suddenly, in the voice of someone who wasn't entirely sure if that was a good thing.

'Hard not to like you,' Rhazha said into her drink, just this side of sarcastic. 'Everyone likes the quiet ones.'

Fenwick launched into a new song—something heroic and tuneless. His voice cracked like a teenage boy being chased by ghosts.

Adanion winced. 'That boy needs fewer chords and more silence.'

'I think he's improving,' Kril said.

They stared at him.

'What?' he added, defensive. 'The chorus almost rhymed this time.'

Across the room, Lila hopped onto the edge of the bar and whispered something to the barman, who rolled his eyes and reached beneath the counter.

Adanion narrowed his own. 'She's either about to order something illegal or summon a dancing bear.'

'She's fun,' Kril said, more to himself than anyone else.

Rhazha looked at Adanion over the rim of her mug. 'You going to warn him?'

'What, that falling for a halfling in a backwater tavern never ends in quiet retirement? That she's probably got three knives strapped to each thigh and a husband locked in a cupboard somewhere?'

'Something like that.'

Adanion shrugged. 'What's life without a few bruises?'

Kril was too busy watching Lila dance back over, holding a tray with what looked suspiciously like flaming shots and two spoons.

'Whatever happens,' Rhazha murmured, 'we're getting a story out of it.'

Adanion smiled. 'At least Fenwick'll have something to write about that doesn't make our ears weep.'

Kril sat up straighter as Lila reached them. She placed the

tray down with a flourish that would've made a theatre troupe jealous.

'Three drinks,' she declared, 'two spoons, and one highly questionable dessert.'

Rhazha leaned forward. 'Is that... on fire?'

Lila grinned. 'Only slightly.'

The dessert was a bowl of thick, melted chocolate spiked with cinnamon and, judging by the smell, something that could power siege engines. Toasted sweetbread floated in it like innocent victims. The spoons gleamed.

'I saw you watching me,' Lila said, turning to Kril. 'So now you get to try my favourite thing in the world.'

He reached cautiously for a spoon. 'Burning pudding?'

'Close.' She winked. 'Dangerous dessert. And company that doesn't pretend to be braver than they are.'

Kril blinked. 'That's oddly specific.'

'I'm an oddly specific person.'

She scooped a bite and ate it with closed eyes, savouring every second. When she opened them again, she tilted her spoon towards him. 'Come on, big man. The pudding won't slay itself.'

Kril frowned at the dessert like it had shown up late to war and brought fruit salad. 'I thought pudding had rules.'

Across the table, Adanion leaned to Rhazha. 'I'm starting to like her.'

Kril tried it. His eyebrows rose half a degree.

'That's good,' he muttered.

'It's excellent,' Lila corrected. 'And the trick is to let the spice sneak up on you.'

He nodded solemnly, as if she'd explained a sacred rite.

They talked for a while—about nothing and everything. Lila told stories of Mudwater: the ghost chicken that haunted the mayor's basement; the bridge troll who ran a card game on Tuesdays; the annual pie fight that served as both a festival and a subtle town-wide cleansing ritual. Kril listened like someone hearing a lullaby from a place he'd never dared imagine.

Rhazha leaned back in her chair and sighed. 'Alright. I'm off to threaten the bard.'

Adanion gave a small bow. 'Give him my regards. And tell him the E string is flat.'

She wandered towards Fenwick, muttering something about tuning and treason.

Kril watched her go, then turned to Lila. 'You're... different.'

'I'm short,' she corrected. 'And lovely. And very good at darts. Want to see?'

He looked at her in surprise. 'Now?'

'Of course now. Life doesn't wait.'

She hopped down from the table and pulled him with her before he could decide. They crossed to the dartboard where a handful of locals were already playing, and she was immediately welcomed like a cousin returning from battle. Kril stayed behind her, looming awkwardly.

'Watch and learn,' she said, tossing a dart underhand. It thudded neatly into the outer ring.

'That's not the middle,' Kril noted.

She winked at him again. 'No. That's your turn.'

Kril took the dart, weighed it in his hand like a weapon, and threw. It embedded itself in the ceiling beam with a solid thunk.

The room went silent.

'That was... unexpected,' said one of the locals.

'I liked it,' Lila said brightly. 'Artistic interpretation.'

They laughed, and the tavern moved on, as taverns do. Another dart was handed to Kril with reverence.

From the bar, Adanion watched it all unfold with a slow, amused shake of his head.

Fenwick leaned over. 'Do you think this ends with him married, stabbed, or recruited into a halfling circus?'

'All three,' Adanion said. 'But in a way, I think he needs it.'

Back at the dartboard, Kril took another throw—this time aiming lower. The dart hit the board. Lila clapped like it was a royal triumph.

'Well done!' she beamed.

Kril looked at her, then down at his boots. Kril smiled—just barely—but it was the kind of smile that meant something had shifted.

'He's going to crush her,' Rhazha muttered.

Adanion's smile curled. 'If she's lucky.'

From behind the bar, a tankard exploded.

Ale geysered upwards in a spectacular arc, dousing a trio of farmers mid-toast. The bard—Fenwick, naturally—had attempted a dramatic flourish with his lute, which had somehow triggered a nearby bar stool to collapse, which in turn had knocked over a tray of drinks, which then dislodged a precariously balanced chandelier rope.

Adanion ducked, dodged a mug, and caught a flying sausage on the point of his dagger.

The Howling Tankard erupted into absolute chaos.

'Bloody hell,' Rhazha muttered, leaping to her feet as a chair narrowly missed her head.

Kril instinctively placed himself between Lila and the fray, stepping in front of her like a boulder taking offence. 'Is this normal?'

'For him?' Adanion called, gesturing to Fenwick as the

bard attempted to calm an enraged barmaid using what sounded like a romantic ode to pickled turnips. 'Entirely.'

Lila peeked around Kril's arm and whistled. 'That's Mags. She's not going to forgive this until someone bleeds.'

The bartender—a thick-armed woman with the expression of someone who regularly fought bears for recreation—was wielding a ladle like a war hammer.

'Oi!' she bellowed. 'Who knocked my pickled eggs into the fire?!'

A moment of stillness, and then a sheepish voice: 'I sneezed.'

'No one asked why, Fenwick!' Adanion shouted as he sidestepped a stool.

Rhazha rolled up her sleeves with an audible sigh. 'Right. Who's betting on how long before the town guard shows up?'

'Three minutes,' said Adanion.

'Two,' said Kril.

'One and a half,' Lila added cheerfully.

'IF they arrive at all,' Rhazha amended.

'You!' snarled Mags, catching a wayward goblin by the scruff as it tried to make off with a purse.

'No thieving on Tuesdays.'

'It's Wednesday!' the goblin squeaked.

'Exactly,' Mags said, and flung him out the door.

Rhazha blinked. 'What happens on Tuesdays?'

'Better you don't ask,' muttered Adanion.

Meanwhile, Fenwick had somehow positioned himself atop a barrel, strumming furiously.

'I call this one "Ballad of the Broken Bar Stool!" It's still a work in progress—'

'IT HAD BETTER STAY THAT WAY,' Mags roared, charging him.

He squealed and ducked, but the ladle slammed into the

barrel, sending Fenwick flying backwards into the arms of a surprised Faeluran woman, his lute clutched to his chest like a shield.

She did not drop him. In fact, she adjusted her grip, one hand splayed comfortably across his back, claws dimpling the fabric of his shirt—careful, but not apologetic.

'Ooh,' she murmured, tail curling lazily around one ankle. 'You're lighter than I expected.'

Fenwick blinked, acutely aware of how close her face suddenly was. 'You're... not going to hit me?'

Her lips curved, sharp just enough to be interesting. 'Not unless you ask nicely,' she purred.

He promptly forgot how to speak.

Adanion clapped once, loudly. 'Right! Attention! Attention, everyone who hasn't suffered a head injury—may I suggest a proper tavern contest? Something not destructive?'

There was a suspicious lull. A goat bleated somewhere near the hearth. A half-orc holding two steins scratched his chin.

'What sort of contest?' asked Mags, ladle dripping, eyebrow cocked.

Adanion grinned. 'A musical duel. Fenwick versus... anyone brave enough.'

'I accept!' shouted a voice that sounded like a rusted pan scraping down stone steps.

A figure stood from the shadows: a dwarf with wild eyes and a lute covered in questionable stains. She cracked her knuckles. The room groaned.

'Oh dear gods,' Fenwick whispered. 'That's Iron-Toothed Beryl.'

Adanion's eyes twinkled. 'Perfect. Someone fetch the drum.'

The crowd rearranged itself into a semi-circle around a rickety wooden table repurposed as a stage. Fenwick stood at one end, still slightly stunned from being flirted with. Beryl stood at the other, fingers twitching like they were trying to strangle her instrument into submission.

Mags crossed her arms. 'Rules are simple. Best song wins. Worst song... drinks the Goblet.'

A collective shudder. The Goblet was infamous—containing whatever Mags had found under the bar last week, plus one pickled egg and a shot of regret.

Fenwick looked to Adanion. 'Do I have to win?'

'Just don't lose,' Adanion said. 'Kril, sit near him. If he starts crying, throw something.'

'I don't cry in public,' Fenwick said, strumming a slightly less off-key chord.

'You will, once you hear Beryl,' Lila said, nudging Kril.

Rhazha leaned back, already polishing an axe. 'Well. At least it's not goblins this time.'

'You say that,' Adanion muttered, eyeing the rafters.

Beryl played first.

It was... indescribable. Not in the poetic sense—more in the 'may the gods have mercy on your eardrums' sense. It began like a love song but rapidly devolved into what sounded like a screaming cat trapped in a brass drum.

Someone wept openly. A gnome fell asleep out of self-defence.

Near the fireplace, Lila laughed so hard she nearly dropped her drink. Her cheeks were flushed from both ale and amusement, and her curls bounced wildly with each giggle. She was slender but clearly strong, the kind of woman who looked like she could climb a tree faster than most men could fall out of one. Her green blouse clung in all the right places, making it abundantly clear she was blessed in the chest department—but there was nothing exaggerated about her. Just soft curves, a dancer's poise, and the kind of confidence that made people turn when she walked into a room.

Kril had definitely noticed.

Then it was Fenwick's turn.

He cleared his throat. Strummed once. Twice. Found the chord.

And then—

He played.

It wasn't perfect. It wasn't clean. But there was something in it. A little bit of longing. A little bit of laughter. A tale of fools, ghosts, halflings, bar fights, and one towering warrior who didn't know how to dance.

When he finished, no one clapped.

They cheered.

Mags sniffed once. 'It's not terrible,' she admitted.

Kril thumped Fenwick on the back hard enough to nearly knock him off the table. 'You survived.'

'Barely,' Fenwick wheezed.

Lila leaned closer to Kril, voice low and teasing. 'I think he's going to get laid.'

Kril blinked. 'Is that the reward?'

She smirked. 'Sometimes the real reward walks in late, sits by the hearth… and doesn't even know he's being hunted.'

Kril looked genuinely puzzled. 'Who's hunting?'

Lila laughed softly and leaned back, eyes twinkling. *'Exactly.'*

They settled back near the hearth as the tavern slowly regained some semblance of order. Fenwick was gifted a beer and a pat on the head by the gnome, Beryl was nursing a wounded ego and a mug of the Goblet's wrath, and Adanion was deep in whispered conversation with Rhazha near the bar.

Lila rested her chin on her hand. 'So. Kril.'

He turned.

She smiled. 'Ask me nicely, and I'll see about a second round.'

A pause.

Then she winked.

Kril's ears turned faintly red.

He looked at her. Then down at his boots again.

And smiled.

Just a bit more than before.

The tavern's chatter returned, blending with the creak of floorboards and the steady thrum of Fenwick's off-key lute. Outside, the moon hung over Mudwater like a breath held too long.

Kril leaned against the wall, Lila beside him—quiet, present, and more grounding than any anchor he'd known. For once, he wasn't just the mountain in the room. Just a man, with muddy boots and a heart that hadn't quite calmed down.

'So,' Lila said, nudging him with her elbow, 'you ever think you'd be the dancing type?'

He snorted. 'No. Not really.'

She grinned, eyes dancing. 'Well. Maybe you're full of surprises.'

He looked at her. And this time, he didn't look away.

Across the room, Rhazha nodded towards them, sipping her drink. 'She's going to be trouble.'

Adanion smirked. 'Let's hope so.'

The night stretched out before them, thick with the scent of ale and possibility.

And for the first time in a long time, Kril was looking forward to the dawn.

CHAPTER SIX

The Caravan And The Code

They were back on the road the next morning, heads pounding with the dull hammer of last night's ale, mouths dry as old parchment, and none of them willing to admit just how bad the hangover really was. Adanion rode at the front, reins loose in one hand, whistling a jaunty little tune that bounced off the early dawn like a cheerful lie. The sound did nothing to soothe Kril's pounding skull—it only made it worse, a sharp reminder of every poorly judged drink and misplaced joke. Yet Adanion was still grinning like a man who'd discovered a sack of gold buried beneath his bedroll, the kind of grin that promised trouble and delight in equal measure. The breeze tugged at his cloak, stirring loose strands of hair, and even the tired clatter of hooves seemed to keep rhythm with his careless whistle.

A squirrel darted across the path ahead of them, its tail high and bushy with indignation. Kril's horse snorted at the sudden movement, but he didn't flinch—just narrowed his eyes like the very existence of wildlife was a personal affront to his hangover.

They'd left Mudwater behind before the sun had fully lifted its head above the horizon. The last few revellers still slumped over tavern benches, and the street dogs had yet to stir from their sleeping spots beneath carts and porches. The village's air still held the faint scent of last night's fires and fried meat, now soured by the memory of too much ale. Their horses picked along the muddy road with patient hooves, steam rising from their flanks with each snort of cold air. A few lone crows circled overhead, their calls hollow against the pale sky. Mud clung to the horses' fetlocks, and frost clung stubbornly to the weeds at the roadside.

'You'd think he slept with Iron-Toothed Beryl,' Rhazha muttered.

Kril visibly shuddered.

Adanion only grinned. 'She did offer. But I'm too young to die.'

'You know, modesty is still free in most provinces.' Rhazha added, trotting up beside him.

Adanion winked. 'Just enjoying the finer things in life, my dear. Unlike our towering companion, who still looks like he's processing what a goodbye peck on the cheek means.'

Behind them, Kril shifted in his saddle. He'd been unusually quiet since they left Mudwater, his usual gravelly rumble of a voice silent. The halfling's kiss had stunned him more than any battle wound.

'She was... bold,' he said finally.

'And bouncy, hm?' added Adanion, with a chuckle.

Rhazha laughed aloud, loud enough to startle a nearby crow from a fence post. 'And yet she brought you to your knees, Kril. Figuratively speaking.'

Kril frowned. 'I didn't kneel.'

Adanion glanced back, smirking. 'Not yet.'

Rhazha shook her head, amused despite herself. There was something comforting about the way the two of them bickered—like old stones grinding together, predictable and oddly grounding. For all their differences, they had a rhythm.

A pattern. One she was starting to recognise.

They rode on, the morning sun rising behind them, casting long shadows across the frost-bitten road. The chill of early autumn was beginning to settle in, turning the leaves amber and gold, the wind crisp with the promise of colder days ahead. The banter quieted as the miles passed beneath their horses' hooves.

Ahead, the road curved through a shallow valley where mist still clung to the ground, low and silver. Birds scattered as they passed, and a fox bolted into the underbrush with a flash of red tail. The quiet was deeper here, but not empty—filled with the gentle rustle of leaves, the steady creak of saddle leather, and the whispering hush of breath in the cold.

There was something soothing about the rhythm of the journey, even with the headache. The way the trees arched overhead in lazy rows, the way the frost cracked faintly beneath the weight of hooves—it all had the quiet patience of the road. Birds called from high branches, their songs sharp and fleeting. Now and then, a squirrel darted through the underbrush, tail flicking. The smell of damp earth and woodsmoke hung in the air, grounding and familiar.

Adanion whistled a new tune, slower this time, almost thoughtful.

Rhazha rode with one hand on the reins and the other resting on the hilt of a throwing knife. She didn't say much. Her gaze shifted often, watching the tree line, the road behind, the sky above. She didn't trust silence for long—not when she'd lived too many years learning how quickly peace could break.

Kril, for his part, rode like a statue on horseback. Upright. Unflinching. His axe hung at his side, the leather strap of its sling creaking softly with every stride. He hadn't spoken again. That one small kiss had turned the big man inward, thoughts hidden behind his usual stone-faced stare.

They made a strange trio, she thought—a smiling rogue, a silent wall, and an orc with a past she didn't care to name just yet. And yet, here they were, moving forward together. For now.

They might've kept riding in silence had it not been for the smoke.

The smell reached them before the full sight did—a biting tang of ash and burnt wood that soured the back of the throat. The horses grew restless beneath them, ears flicking, hooves stamping uncertainly on the road. Rhazha tightened her grip on the reins, eyes narrowing as she leaned forward in the saddle.

It curled in the sky like a dark finger, rising above the treetops just off the road. Too much for a cooking fire. Too close for comfort.

'That's not a campfire,' she said, sitting up straighter.

Even without the words, the tension between them shifted, like the sudden stillness before a storm. Kril shifted in his saddle, his hand already resting on the axe at his hip. His brow furrowed as he stared at the smoke, watching how it moved—rising in heavy coils instead of drifting freely. Controlled fire didn't billow like that. This was something wild. Violent.

'Could be a village,' he rumbled, voice low, cautious.

'Or a caravan,' Adanion added, already tugging his horse into a canter.

They spurred their mounts into a gallop, hooves pounding the earth with urgent rhythm. The trees on either side blurred past as the road bent sharply ahead, the smoke growing thicker, closer, curling tighter into the sky like a clenched fist.

Even without speaking, they all sensed it now—a tension sharp enough to cut, thick in the air like breath held too long. The breeze carried not only the acrid scent of burning but something fouler beneath it: charred leather, scorched meat, the bitter tang of fear, prickling along the skin.

Then, just as they rounded the bend—

Carnage.

A merchant caravan had been ambushed at the roadside. The scene erupted into their view all at once—the acrid sting of smoke and burnt wood clawing at their senses, the haze casting the morning in an ugly, coppery light. One wagon burned fiercely, flames licking at the sky and turning the sunlight to a sickly, flickering orange. The crackle of fire mingled with the sharper notes of destruction: the creak of collapsing wood, the sharp crash of broken glass, the occasional scream from a wounded beast of burden still tangled in its harness.

The other wagons had fared no better. Half-ransacked, their cargo lay strewn across the dirt in ruined heaps—crushed crates, torn fabrics, and broken boxes of spices whose contents drifted like coloured dust in the wind. A barrel of wine had burst open, its red stain soaking into the earth like blood.

Rhazha muttered a curse under her breath. Her eyes darted, cataloguing the wreckage.

Among it all, six gnolls prowled like hyena-faced nightmares, savage and twitching with animal hunger. Their patchwork armour clinked with bone and rusted iron, and their movements had the erratic energy of something half-starved and wholly cruel. One slouched against a smouldering cart, urinating carelessly on a once-beautiful tapestry, its yellow stain spreading like a blight. Another gnawed on a child's toy—a wooden horse carved with careful hands—splinters catching on its jagged teeth. The toy crunched and snapped. The gnoll tossed it aside with a snort.

Adanion didn't wait.

He glanced at Kril—no words, just a nod. The big man returned it, silent and steady.

Then Adanion drew his sword with a metallic whisper and kicked his horse forward.

'No time to argue. Hit hard. Hit fast.'

Rhazha was right behind him, leaping off her horse mid-motion, twin axes in hand.

Kril dismounted less gracefully—a grunt, a stomp—and hit the ground like an avalanche. He let out a bellow that made the nearest gnoll whirl around just in time to catch a backhand, smashing it into a burning cart.

Adanion was just behind him, sliding from his mount with a blade in hand, while Rhazha dropped lightly to the ground a few paces to Kril's right, axes ready.

The fight exploded with savage fury.

The charge was sudden—a blur of motion and steel.

Leaping past a toppled wagon on Kril's left, Adanion's sword flashed in perfect timing with Kril's blow, intercepting a gnoll that would have struck the big man's flank. His blade found a throat before the creature even had time to snarl, blood spraying in a bright arc as he spun past. The next one lunged with a jagged spear, but he ducked under it, slashing low to hamstring it with a precise, fluid strike. He didn't pause. Didn't need to. His movements were measured, elegant, born of years surviving long odds. If the gnolls were wild, he was colder—trained, disciplined, surgical.

Rhazha crashed into the fray with a shout, all momentum

and instinct. She slammed the heel of her boot into a gnoll's kneecap, sending it toppling sideways before burying her axe in the exposed ribs. She spun around the rear of Kril's position, twin axes ready, cutting off any gnoll attempting to circle past him, while Adanion engaged another to the left.

Another one howled and barrelled towards her, swinging a crude club made from knotted iron and bone. She ducked, rolled beneath it, and slashed both weapons upwards—one into the thigh, the other arcing up into the gut. Blood sprayed as the beast buckled, screaming, before she kicked it aside and moved on.

One of the gnolls—taller, broader across the shoulders, with one ear torn clean off—bellowed a command in a guttural bark. The others responded like feral dogs on a leash: turning, snapping, refocusing on the threat. This one was no scavenger. It had led the attack, judging by the crude bangles of teeth and trinkets that clattered across its chest like trophies. Its yellow eyes locked on Kril, and it raised a wicked-looking cleaver of chipped stone and iron.

Adanion darted to the leader gnoll's right, forcing it to split its attention, while Rhazha moved to cover Kril's back, axes braced for any strike from behind.

Kril didn't flinch. The big man surged forward with a growl that rumbled low in his chest. The charging gnoll brought its weapon down in a heavy arc—Kril caught the blow on his forearm guard and stepped into the creature's reach, slamming a brutal elbow into its jaw. Bone cracked. The gnoll staggered, and Kril followed with a devastating overhead blow from his axe that split its shoulder and sent it crumpling to the earth.

He didn't stop moving. Another gnoll leapt onto his back, claws raking at his shoulders. Kril roared, reached behind him, and flung the attacker over his shoulder like a sack of grain. It landed hard—dazed—and he stomped its throat before it could rise.

Rhazha moved like a tempest unleashed—low, fast, and deadly. Her twin axes whirled through the air in a blur, each strike a precise, brutal incision meant to maim or kill. She ducked beneath a gnoll's savage swipe, spinning with balletic grace, then slammed an axe deep into its ribs. The creature's laughter turned to choking gurgles as it crumpled to the ground. Adanion was no less a force—he danced through the fray with the fluid elegance of a duellist at a noble's ball. His feet barely touched the earth as he slipped under wild swipes and countered with sharp, calculated strikes. His sword flashed, finding gaps in the gnolls' ragged defences, slitting throats and severing tendons with merciless efficiency.

Kril, by contrast, was a juggernaut of raw power. He didn't dance; he crushed.

The three moved as a compact unit: Kril the centre of the storm, Adanion slicing along the left, Rhazha sweeping the right, their attacks overlapping and keeping the gnolls off balance.

With a roar, he grabbed a gnoll by the scruff, lifting it high overhead before hurling it into another with a sickening crash of snarling limbs. Another charged him head-on, jaws bared and claws extended. Kril met it with a bone-shattering shoulder tackle, the impact echoing like a hammer on steel. The gnoll staggered back, stunned, blood spurting from shattered ribs.

A fourth gnoll tried to slip around them—fast, skittish, looking to flee or flank. Rhazha's eyes caught it immediately to Kril's far right. One axe hurled end-over-end, finding its mark, while Adanion's dagger cut down another as it tried to flee towards the treeline. The creature shrieked, legs giving way, and collapsed into a heap of twitching limbs.

A MODERATE CHANCE OF SCREAMING

Two gnolls broke, racing for the treeline. Adanion's dagger flew true, sinking deep between the shoulder blades of one just as it reached the edge of the road. The other was no match for Rhazha, who caught it with deadly precision, dragging it down in a swift, merciless end.

The battlefield fell silent but for the crackle of the dying fire and the heavy breathing of those left standing—the storm passed, but the price clear in every broken crate and spilt treasure.

The air hung heavy with the acrid bite of smoke and sweat, the stench of burnt wood and singed leather clawing at their nostrils. Around them, the broken remnants of the ambush—splintered wagon wheels, scattered goods, and crushed crates—lay silent under a sky that seemed too wide and empty now. For a moment, the battlefield felt frozen, as if even the wind dared not disturb the uneasy peace that had settled. Each of them caught their breath, muscles still taut, eyes scanning for any sign that the fight might flare up again. But the gnolls were truly gone, leaving only the quiet aftermath—and the weight of what had just been done.

The smoke still rose, and the fire still crackled, but the only sounds now were the whimpers of shaken merchants and the occasional sob.

Kril stood in the middle of it all, blood drying on his knuckles, soot streaked across his rugged face like war paint. His breath came slow and heavy, chest rising and falling with the weight of the fight now past but not yet forgotten. Suddenly, a small figure broke through the haze—a child no older than six, trembling, with tear-streaked cheeks and a tunic so filthy it might have once been white. She ran without hesitation, arms flung wide, and clung to Kril's leg like he was the last solid thing in a world gone mad. Her sobs were quiet but insistent, a fragile sound that cut through the chaos. For a long moment, Kril simply froze—the rough edges of battle softened by the smallness and vulnerability of this unexpected presence. Then, very slowly, his massive hand lowered to rest gently on the child's back, steady and sure. She did not let go. In that fragile hold, beneath the smoke and ruin, something unspoken passed between them—a stubborn promise that she would be protected.

A squat, soot-covered dwarf limped over, coughing from the smoke. His beard was singed at the ends. He held one arm close to his ribs.

'Damn beasts came outta nowhere,' he grunted. 'Didn't think we'd make it. You lot...'

He trailed off, his eyes on the corpses.

'You saved us.'

Adanion wiped his blade clean and sheathed it. 'You're welcome.'

The dwarf reached into a pouch and pulled out a small sack of coin. 'Not much, but it's yours.'

Adanion held up a hand. 'We're already on a job. Keep it.'

The dwarf frowned. 'You sure?'

Kril gently pried the child from his leg and knelt so they were eye-level. 'You should stay near your people,' he rumbled softly.

She nodded, wide-eyed, and scampered off.

Rhazha crossed her arms. 'You two always stop to help like this?'

Adanion shrugged. 'Only when people need it.'

She looked at him for a long moment. 'You've got a code.'

He glanced at Kril, who was helping one of the merchants upright a toppled crate. 'We've got each other.'

For a moment, Rhazha said nothing. She just watched the way the child clung to her mother now, the way the dwarf looked at Kril with wary gratitude, the way Adanion took his time checking on everyone before mounting up again.

They weren't just killers. They were something else. Something steadier. Something better.

She'd lived by a code once, long ago.

But look where that had gotten her.

This felt different.

Less about rules, and more about choice.

She turned away before they could see her expression.

She mounted up last, boots finding the stirrups with the ease of habit, but her shoulders were tighter than before. The road ahead was quiet again, the smoke and ruin shrinking behind them with every hoofbeat, but the silence they carried now felt different—not the empty hush of watchfulness, but something more thoughtful. More human.

Adanion rode a little closer to her than before, close enough that she could feel the occasional shift of his horse beside hers. He didn't say anything at first, and she was grateful for it. Words would've ruined the fragile shape of the moment.

Kril rode behind them, axe still strapped and jaw set, but his posture had softened just slightly. Less rigid. Less haunted.

The sun was higher now, gilding the road in faint warmth, though the chill still clung to the shadows. Leaves crunched beneath their horses' hooves, and somewhere in the distance a hawk cried—sharp and sudden—before all went quiet again.

After a long while, Adanion spoke. His voice was low, not

quite a question. 'That girl... she reminded me of someone.'

Rhazha didn't answer right away. Her gaze stayed on the horizon. 'They always do.'

He glanced sideways at her. 'You've done this before. Seen it, lived it.'

'Too many times.'

Kril caught up, his heavy horse matching their pace. 'Makes it harder,' he said. 'Not easier.'

Rhazha let out a slow breath. 'Still worth doing?'

Kril nodded once. 'Every time.'

Adanion didn't add anything to that—just looked ahead, his mouth set in a thoughtful line. The road stretched on in silence again, but it no longer felt like they were avoiding something. It felt more like they'd said what needed saying, and the rest could be carried quietly.

They kept riding until the sun dipped low behind the trees, painting the sky in amber and violet. The world narrowed to hoofbeats, breath, and the quiet bond of three people who'd been tempered, just a little more, by what they'd faced together.

They rode on after that, slower now, the silence between them no longer empty. The air had changed. There was an unspoken weight to what they'd done, but also a strange kind of lightness. They had made a choice. And that mattered.

They made camp in a hollow not far from the road, tucked between leaning trees and the low murmur of a creek. The fire crackled quietly, its warmth pushing back the night as stars blinked into the sky, pale and watchful.

No one said much at first.

Kril sat with his axe across his knees, sharpening it in slow, steady strokes. Adanion leaned back on one elbow, watching the flames flicker, his sword nearby but untouched. Rhazha sat a little apart, legs crossed, arms wrapped loosely around her knees. She stared into the fire like it might answer something.

Finally, she spoke.

'You ever lose anyone?' Her voice was low, almost casual, but it didn't fool either of them.

Kril didn't look up. 'Yes.'

Adanion nodded, still watching the fire. 'More than I can count.'

She was quiet for a moment. 'Me too.'

The wind rustled through the trees. Somewhere in the dark, a nightbird called once, then fell silent.

Kril slid the whetstone back into his pack. 'That's why we help,' he said. 'So fewer people have to say that.'

Rhazha looked at him. He wasn't trying to be profound. Just honest.

She nodded once.

'I can work with that.'

Adanion smiled faintly. 'Sounds like you understand it.'

For a while, the only sound was the crackle of fire and the slow, steady breathing of three people who, for the first time, didn't feel like strangers.

They still had a long way to go. But for now, they had the road, the fire, and each other.

The quiet lingered as the fire settled into a bed of coals. Most of the caravan had turned in, though a few low voices still murmured at the edges of the camp. Kril reached for a stick and began tracing idle shapes in the dirt.

'You ever think about stopping?' he asked after a while, not looking at either of them. 'Not just a break. I mean—

properly stopping. Hanging up the sword. Letting the world spin on without you.'

Rhazha tilted her head, watching him. 'That ever really work for someone like you?'

He gave a noncommittal grunt. 'Sometimes I think I could find a quiet place. Build something. Farm, maybe.'

Adanion laughed softly. 'You? Milking goats and planting turnips?'

Kril's mouth tugged into something that might've been a smile. 'A man can dream.'

Rhazha didn't answer right away. She thought of the road behind them—dust and blood and fire. She thought of her father's hands, steady on a blade, and the code he'd passed down like a birthright.

'Stopping sounds simple until you try it,' she said finally. 'The world doesn't let you walk away clean.'

Adanion poked at the fire with a charred stick. 'Aye. And sometimes, the kind of folk who can do what we did today… they're the same ones who can't leave it behind.'

'Doesn't mean we don't want to,' Kril said.

A silence followed—not awkward, just full. Comfortable, in its way. The kind that came when people had shared danger and lived to speak of it.

A soft rustle broke it: one of the caravan's children, no more than six or seven, toddled near the fire, rubbing sleep from her eyes. Rhazha's hand went to her belt automatically, fingers brushing the hilt of her knife—old habits dying hard—then relaxed when she recognised the girl.

The child didn't speak. She simply padded over to Rhazha, leaned against her leg, and curled up there, head resting on folded arms.

Rhazha blinked. Then, very slowly, she let her hand fall away from the blade and placed it gently on the girl's back.

'Looks like you've got a shadow,' Adanion said softly.

'Hmph.' Rhazha didn't smile, but something in her eyes warmed. 'She'll get bored of me by morning.'

But she didn't move. And the fire burned low.

The night deepened, and still no one moved to sleep. The fire's glow painted long shadows on their faces, flickering gently with every breeze. Somewhere beyond the hollow, a fox barked once—sharp and quick—then silence again. It wasn't fear that kept them awake, nor even the echo of the fight, but something quieter, more difficult to name. The aftermath of violence always left a space behind, hollow as a wound.

Adanion stretched out his legs with a sigh and tossed a twig into the fire. 'You think the girl'll be all right?' he asked.

Kril gave a slow nod. 'She's got her people. That's more than some get.'

Rhazha shifted slightly, resting her chin on her knee. 'She'll remember today. Might not know what it means yet, but she'll remember it.'

'That's the trouble with surviving,' Adanion muttered. 'You never forget who stepped in... or who didn't.'

They fell quiet again, each with their own ghosts. The kind that didn't rattle chains or scream in the night, but whispered at the edge of memory, waiting to be noticed.

A log collapsed in the fire, sending up a small shower of sparks. Rhazha blinked slowly, eyes tracking the embers. 'I used to think it was all chance,' she said. 'Who lives. Who dies. Who ends up with blood on their boots and who walks away clean.'

'And now?' Kril asked.

She shrugged. 'Now I think maybe the road has its own sort of justice. You choose which way to go. And if you're lucky, you don't walk it alone.'

Adanion gave a small, crooked smile. 'You're getting philosophical in your old age.'

'I'm not old.'

'No, but you're brooding by firelight and waxing poetic about fate. That's halfway to a grey beard and a pipe.'

Rhazha threw a pinecone at him. It bounced off his shoulder. He caught it on the second toss and held it up triumphantly.

'There's the warrior I've come to know,' he grinned.

'Don't get used to it,' she said. But there was no bite in it. Only the easy warmth of shared firelight and the slow stitching of something like trust.

CHAPTER SEVEN

FIRELIGHT, FLIRTATION, AND THE FIRST HINT OF TROUBLE

C AMP THAT NIGHT WAS QUIET.
The trees pressed close, dark silhouettes against the deep navy sky, their leaves rustling with secrets they had no interest in sharing. A thin breeze stirred embers from the fire, sending occasional sparks dancing like fireflies into the night. Somewhere far off, an owl called once—then silence.

Above, the stars scattered cold and unblinking across the heavens, distant and unmoved by the mortal efforts playing out beneath them. The moon, only a sliver, cast a faint silver sheen over the treetops, just enough to make the shadows seem deeper by comparison. Everything in the forest felt half-held—like the world itself was listening.

It had been hours since the fight, but the scent of scorched fur and blood still lingered faintly in the back of their throats, carried on the wind like an unwelcome memory. The caravan lay far behind them now, but not far enough to forget. Not yet.

Kril snored, slumped against a tree with one massive arm draped over his axe like a child clutching a favourite toy.

The haft stretched across his lap, scratched and darkened from their earlier brawl with the gnolls. One boot had come off somewhere—probably flung during combat, or perhaps sheer defiance of footwear. He didn't stir. His snores came in rhythmic bursts, oddly peaceful for a man who'd spent the afternoon turning monsters into meat paste.

The fire snapped again. A soft pop, followed by the hiss of sap burning off bark. Shadows danced along the trees like restless ghosts. Even the breeze seemed to tread lightly here, slipping between the trunks as though trying not to wake the forest.

A cricket chirped somewhere nearby, then fell silent. The fire crackled softly in the middle of their small camp, casting flickering shadows across packs and bedrolls. The tension of the day hadn't fully faded—just sunk deeper, like coals banked beneath ash.

Rhazha sat near the fire, legs stretched out, her fingers drawing a whetstone slow and sure along the curve of her axe. *Schrrrk. Schrrrk.* Sparks flickered and died, each pass as deliberate as a lover's stroke. The firelight turned her amber eyes to molten gold, her expression unreadable but far from soft. Her twin axes rested within arm's reach, gleaming and sharpened. Her leathers clung in all the right ways, scarred but supple, the tension in her shoulders coiled rather than tired. Just like her—polished, dangerous, and ready to bite.

Around her, the camp was orderly, but not rigid. Her gear was stacked where it could be grabbed quickly; her bedroll sat untouched, though the blanket had been shaken out and spread in readiness. Everything about her said she'd done this a hundred times before. Maybe more.

She didn't fidget. Didn't hum. Just that same steady motion, blade to stone, methodical as a heartbeat. Her breathing was slow and even, but her shoulders never quite dropped. Not even now. Rest didn't come easy to people like her—not unless it was earned.

Adanion poured wine from a leather skin, the liquid catching the firelight as he offered her a cup. His sleeves were rolled back, his forearms still smudged faintly with dried blood and soot. He moved without tension, but not lazily—just fluid, the way a river moved around stone.

She took it, silently.

They sat in a moment of companionable nothingness—no threats, no urgent plans, just the warmth of a fire and the crackle of wood burning slow. The kind of peace that felt borrowed, not gifted. Temporary. Fragile.

'You're not what I expected,' she said at last.

Adanion took a sip of his own drink. 'You expected a smug, self-absorbed pretty boy who sleeps with everything that moves?'

She raised an eyebrow. 'You knew that?'

'I'm very self-aware. It's part of my charm.'

She smirked, but didn't reply.

He stretched his legs towards the fire, letting the warmth ease the stiffness from his thighs. 'But for the record, I sleep with very select people. Not everything. I have standards.'

'Oh, do you?' she asked, mildly amused.

'High ones,' he said, glancing her way. 'I only flirt with people who could kill me.'

'Smart man.'

'Survival instinct.'

She took another sip, watching the flames. 'You're not the worst.'

Adanion placed a hand over his heart in mock offence. 'Be still, my fluttering heart. I live for such praise.'

'Don't get used to it.'

'Too late.'

Adanion let his eyes wander—first to the fire, then to the shadows dancing beyond. He didn't press her, didn't fill the moment with more words than it needed. He could feel the distance between them shift slightly. Not closed, but bridged. A little.

He glanced at her again. 'Why do you want the artefact?'

Her jaw tensed. She looked at the fire like it might give her an excuse not to answer.

'It's not for me,' she said at last, her voice flat, the earlier softness instantly gone. 'It's a delivery. I was hired to make sure it gets where it belongs.'

'You don't strike me as the 'complicated feelings' type.'

'I'm not.'

He nodded slowly. 'But you are the honourable kind. I see that much.'

She gave a half-smile. 'You flirt like it's breathing.'

'Only when I'm interested.'

Their eyes met across the flickering orange light. No grin. No banter. Just an acknowledgement.

Something different. Something rawer than charm.

The moment held—brief, steady, and sharp as a blade's edge. There was no room for masks in that quiet look, no room for pretence. Just two people who had each lost something, who each carried something too heavy to put down. The fire snapped between them, a sharp crack as a log shifted, but neither flinched.

A quiet passed between them, but it wasn't awkward. It was the kind of silence that formed when two people finally ran out of masks and simply… existed near each other.

The fire cracked again, louder this time, casting a sudden flicker of light against the trees. Rhazha didn't flinch, but her eyes narrowed slightly, her hand resting against the haft of her axe for the briefest of moments before easing away. Old habits. She let them guide her, but not define her.

Adanion watched her from the corner of his eye. There was a calmness to her now—measured, deliberate. But he knew that calm was hard-earned, forged in fire and grief, not gifted. It reminded him of old comrades. Ones who didn't live long enough to sit beside a quiet fire.

He sipped his wine again, slower now, letting the heat of it settle through him. 'You don't strike me as someone who trusts easily,' he said, not looking at her.

'I don't,' she replied, without hesitation.

'But you're here. With us.'

Rhazha shrugged. 'You haven't given me reason to walk away yet.'

He smiled faintly. 'That's as good as a compliment from you, I think.'

'Don't push it.'

She said it drily, but not unkind. The edge in her tone had dulled slightly—not submission, but a crack in the wall. A small one. Enough for him to glimpse that maybe, just maybe, she didn't mind the company.

The fire settled into a soft glow, throwing long, orange-gold shadows that danced across Kril's slumped form. His snores rolled on, oddly reassuring. Like thunder in the distance—present, but not threatening.

Adanion placed the wineskin aside and leaned back on his elbows, staring up through a break in the trees. The stars above were scattered like broken glass across deep velvet. Distant. Beautiful. Indifferent.

He felt Rhazha shift beside him but didn't look. 'You've

been quiet about that artefact. Makes me wonder if it's more than just loot.'

'I think people lie. Especially when power's involved.'

'So, are we talking cursed trinket… or world-ending doom charm?'

He glanced at her now, eyebrows raised.

'I'm not here for power, Adanion,' she said, quieter. 'I'm here to help someone reclaim something that should never have been taken. That's it.'

'And when they get it?'

'I walk away.'

He studied her for a moment, as if weighing the truth of her words. There was no doubt in her voice, no hidden agenda he could hear. But something else lingered beneath— regret, maybe. Or guilt.

He didn't press. He just said, 'Then I hope we get there in time.'

Their eyes met across the flickering orange light. No grin. No banter. Just an acknowledgement.

Something different. Something rawer than charm.

Then Kril snorted in his sleep and let out a monumental fart that echoed against the trees like a dying war horn.

Adanion looked towards the heavens. 'Romance is hard with him around.'

Rhazha burst into laughter. 'You two are insane.'

He grinned. 'But we're good at it.'

She shook her head, still chuckling softly, but the sound faded quicker than it should have. The laughter seemed to hang in the air for a moment, then vanished, swallowed by the thick silence of the forest. Her eyes drifted once more towards the trees, scanning the darkness just beyond the fire's fragile glow. The warmth of the flames did little to reach the cold caution settling in her gaze. The laughter didn't linger in her posture—her shoulders stiffened subtly, the faintest crease forming between her brows.

Adanion noticed all of it but said nothing. There was something unspoken in the way she watched the shadows, a tension coiled beneath her skin. It was the same kind of alertness he had learned to wear when walking into a trap—something born of experience, and perhaps, old scars.

The wine was nearly gone, the last embers of the fire sinking lower. The night deepened, folding around the camp like a heavy blanket. Rhazha rose quietly, her movements smooth and deliberate. 'I'm taking first watch,' she said, her voice low, the earlier humour stripped away like old skin. It was a statement, not a request.

'I'll take second,' Adanion replied, setting his cup aside. He watched her for a moment, noting how the moonlight outlined her figure as she stepped away from the fire, half-silhouetted against the dark woods. Her gaze was fixed beyond the camp's edge, eyes methodical and sharp.

She walked with a quiet confidence—light but purposeful steps, each one measured like a predator moving through its territory. There was no softness in her gait, no careless movement. Instead, there was grace, honed through countless nights spent on edge. Control, cold and precise.

Adanion lingered near the dwindling fire, watching her disappear into the shadowed fringe. Her shoulders were squared, not relaxed, as if braced for some unseen threat. Like she was waiting—not just watching, but expecting something. Or someone.

He didn't ask what haunted her thoughts—not yet.

Behind him, Kril shifted in his sleep, mumbling incoherent words while clutching his axe like a trusted companion.

The image might have been comical under different circumstances, but the unease threading through the night kept laughter from finding its way to his lips.

The moon climbed higher, spilling silver light through the thinning canopy. Rhazha's eyes swept the tree line again, slow and methodical, each sweep deliberate and patient. Her fingers rested near the haft of her axe, twitching with a readiness that betrayed years of hard-won survival.

Then she heard it.

A rustle.

Not the random whisper of wind through leaves. Not the faint scurry of a woodland creature.

This was deliberate.

Rhythmic.

Controlled.

Her hand closed around the weapon's grip with a soundless snap. Her muscles coiled—not in panic, but in lethal readiness. Her eyes narrowed, gaze sharpening to a razor edge. She shifted stance, weight settling on the balls of her feet—balanced, poised like a wolf sensing the approach of prey.

Without turning, she spoke softly but firmly. 'Adanion. You might want to wake up.'

'I'm awake,' he said, stepping smoothly to her side, sword already drawn and gleaming faintly in the moonlight. 'You've got your serious face on.'

She gave a faint, dry smile. 'I always have my serious face on.'

'True,' he said, voice low with a hint of wry humour. 'But this one has murder in it.'

She pointed towards the trees. 'Movement. Fast. At least two. Might be scouts.'

'Or thieves,' he replied, tone dropping further, sharpening. His eyes flicked across the shadowed line with practised calm, reading the signs in the shifting branches and disturbed leaves.

Kril groaned behind them, muttering something unintelligible in his sleep before snorting awake. 'If they're not bringing breakfast, send them away,' he grumbled, sitting up and rubbing sleep from his eyes.

Adanion smirked. 'Rise and shine, big guy. We've got company.'

Kril stretched like a mountain uncoiling from slumber, axe ready in his grasp. 'What now?'

The wind shifted suddenly, carrying with it a faint but unmistakable sound—the soft padding of boots on soil. Quiet, but too many for wild animals. Too careful for wandering bandits.

From the shadows stepped three figures, their movements fluid and precise. Black leather hugged their frames, hoods drawn low to obscure faces. They moved like smoke—silent, deliberate, and deadly.

Not goblins. Not bandits. Professionals.

They came without hurry, as though confident the darkness belonged to them. Each step was silent, controlled. These were not common highway cutthroats looking to scavenge from a stray camp. They didn't bother to hide behind trees or scatter in the underbrush. They walked in full view—measured, deliberate, and just close enough to be seen.

Adanion's stance shifted slightly, weight shifting to the balls of his feet. He didn't lift his blade yet, but the edge hung low and ready. Beside him, Rhazha kept one axe in hand, the other still sheathed, fingers drumming lightly against the leather grip. She didn't blink.

Even Kril, half-awake and fully grumpy, squared himself in front of the fire like a bear guarding a den. The air changed. Thickened. As if the forest itself had drawn a breath and was waiting to see who struck first.

The one in front—tall, lean, scar across his cheek—spoke with a calm confidence.

'You three are a long way from anywhere important.'

His voice was smooth, even, like he'd delivered that line a hundred times before. Too calm for someone alone. Which meant he wasn't.

Adanion stepped forward. 'And you're very confident for someone outnumbered.'

The man smiled. 'Am I?'

Another six figures stepped into view. Now they were surrounded.

From every direction, they emerged—silent, practised, fanning out in a wide arc. One dropped down from a tree without a sound. Another knelt beside a bush with a bow already drawn. The firelight caught the gleam of steel in several places. Each figure bore the same dark gear, the same near-featureless armour designed for silence and shadow. No insignia. No colours. Just purpose.

Kril grunted. 'I hate smug ambushes.'

'You hate all ambushes,' Adanion said.

'Fair enough.'

The lead man stepped closer, hands up. 'We're not here to kill you. Just here for what you're after.'

His tone remained friendly, but the implication was sharp. He wasn't here to bargain. He was here to take something. And maybe leave them alive—if they handed it over without trouble.

Adanion cocked his head. 'The artefact?'

The man smiled again. 'You're not the only ones who want it.'

That smile didn't reach his eyes. It wasn't even mockery—it was indifference. He didn't care who they were or what they'd done. Just that they were in the way.

Rhazha stepped forward now, all business. 'Who sent you?'

'Someone with deeper pockets than you.'

She glanced at Adanion without turning her head, barely a flicker of motion, but it was enough. He knew what it meant: Don't wait. Don't talk. These aren't bluffers.

Adanion shrugged. 'Then they overpaid.'

Blades were drawn. The stand-off crackled with tension.

For a breath, no one moved.

The fire snapped.

A breeze whispered through the leaves.

Then Rhazha moved first, axes flashing in an arc of steel. Adanion was already beside her, sword slashing low. Kril roared, charging straight into the largest of them, sending the man flying into a tree with a crack like splintered bone.

The camp erupted.

It was brutal. Fast. Loud.

The attackers were trained—but they hadn't expected this kind of resistance. Not from a campfire trio. Rhazha spun low, sweeping one enemy's legs out from under him and planting a boot in his chest as he fell. Adanion parried two blades at once, twisting one assailant's wrist and driving a knee into his gut. Kril simply cleaved downward, splitting a man's sword and shoulder in one impossibly strong blow.

Steel met steel in a sudden, staccato storm—blades clanging, boots skidding on dirt, breath drawn in sharp gasps between flurries of motion. Arrows flew—two missed, one caught Kril's pauldron with a dull thunk, snapping harmlessly against the metal.

Rhazha ducked beneath a strike, elbowed the attacker in the ribs, and brought her axe down hard on the back of his knee. He screamed—then went still.

Within moments, the tide turned.

And when it was done, two of the attackers lay dead, three groaning on the ground, and the rest fleeing into the night.

Adanion wiped his blade clean against the hem of his tunic, the sharp edge catching the fading glow of the embers. 'That escalated quickly.'

Rhazha turned slowly towards the fallen leader, her eyes cold and unyielding. 'Tell your employer we're not stopping.'

The man coughed, blood glistening on his lips as he struggled to respond. 'You don't know what you're walking into.'

Her voice was steady, hard as steel. 'Neither will they.'

With a quick motion, she knocked him out cold, the sound muffled beneath the crackle of dying fire.

Kril rolled his shoulders, muscles stiff from the sudden fight. 'So. Still think this is just about treasure?'

Adanion's gaze drifted upward, catching the shimmer of stars scattered like shards across the velvet sky. He said quietly, 'No. This is bigger.'

Rhazha glanced towards the stars, their indifferent light casting faint shadows on her face. Then she looked back at the path ahead—dark, uncertain, but calling. 'We move at first light.'

The forest around them settled into a heavy silence, the only sound the faint rustling of leaves moved by a soft breeze. By the time the fire was nothing but embers, cold and grey, and the night swallowed every trace of the battle, Adanion stood alone on the edge of the camp.

He didn't look at Rhazha, though he knew she was nearby. His voice was barely above a whisper, rough with something unspoken. 'When you get your vengeance... what then?'

She didn't answer.

But in the quiet that followed, they both knew—without saying a word—that the road ahead had just become far more dangerous.

And far more personal.

CHAPTER EIGHT

THE BONECRACK RUINS SMELL LIKE REGRET

T HE NIGHT'S UNEASE CLUNG TO them like a shadow as dawn struggled to break through dense, grey clouds. The earlier skirmish was still fresh in their minds, a stark reminder that safety was fleeting, and enemies lurked closer than ever. Yet the path led onward—towards a place whispered of in wary voices and half-forgotten tales, where history bled into stone, and secrets waited buried beneath layers of dust and decay.

The ruin's silhouette loomed dark and imposing against the oppressive, overcast sky, half-swallowed by clinging ivy and cracked stone. Jagged spikes of broken walls jutted upward like the gnarled fingers of a long-dead giant, clawing towards the heavens in silent despair. A chill wind whispered through the skeletal remains of ancient watchtowers, carrying with it the subtle, earthy tang of moss and rot—a scent that spoke of centuries untouched by living feet.

The path leading up to it had narrowed into a tangle of roots and half-buried stone, forcing the trio to move single file beneath a canopy that seemed to droop lower with every step. Light had long faded under thick cloud cover, leaving the world a wash of bleak, grey silhouettes. Every now and then, a crow called from somewhere unseen, its voice rough as gravel. Even the birds sounded like warnings out here.

They had passed a collapsed bridge earlier—little more than a pile of rubble now, drowned in vines—and had to wade through a wide stretch of river with their gear lifted over their heads. That crossing had taken its toll.

Adanion wiped his brow, the sweat mingling with the grime caked thick on his face. The day's march had proven far harder than he'd expected; the river crossing had left their clothes damp and clinging uncomfortably to their skin. His boots squelched softly against the soft earth as he shuffled forward, every step a reminder of the toll already taken. His thighs ached with each movement, the wet cloth of his trousers chafing where it clung too tightly. The air felt laden now, laced with the thick scent of moss and mildew, and his hand stayed close to the hilt of his sword—not out of habit, but something closer to instinct.

Beside him, Kril grunted softly, hefting his massive axe higher to step over a fallen timber beam. The half-giant's breath was deep and steady, a slow rhythm that steadied his bulk. His usual scowl was softened today by the solemnity of the place. The weight of it settled on all of them.

'Can't say I like this,' Kril muttered, almost to himself. His eyes flicked across the looming shadows of ruined stone and twisted trees, his broad shoulders tense beneath the strap of his pack.

Rhazha's gaze darted to the crumbled entrance ahead. 'We're close,' she murmured, her voice low and reverent. 'The Bonecrack Ruins haven't seen living feet in decades.'

The three halted, and silence fell thick around them, almost as oppressive as the humid air. It pressed in like a living thing, making every breath feel laden. The hush felt unnatural, prickling Adanion's skin like static. It wasn't just the ruins—though they were grim enough. It was the quiet. Too quiet. As if the whole forest was holding its breath, waiting for them to make the next move.

Adanion glanced sideways at Rhazha, curiosity stirring despite the tension. 'What's the story behind the name?' he asked quietly.

She shrugged, a shadow passing across her face. 'A clan war long ago. A massacre so brutal the bones still whisper at night. That's what the elders say.'

Kril spat onto the ground, the sound harsh in the stillness. 'Sounds like the kind of place I'd like to avoid.'

'Too late for that,' Adanion grinned, drawing his sword with a soft hiss of steel. 'After all, the prize is inside.'

Beyond the flickering torchlight, shadows seemed to writhe and twist. A ghostly skittering echoed from deeper within the dark tunnels, making Rhazha's grip tighten on her axes. 'Stay sharp,' she warned. 'This place isn't empty.'

The air was different here—stagnant and bitter, like a place that hadn't breathed in centuries. Every footstep disturbed ancient dust, raising thin clouds that clung to their clothes and throats. The walls seemed to close in the deeper they went, carved stone giving way to natural rock, as if the ruin had grown down into the bones of the earth.

Adanion stepped forward cautiously, eyes sweeping the gloom. His boots made no sound on the soft, dust-covered earth. Kril followed silently, the massive weight of his axe a comforting presence in the claustrophobic darkness.

Above them, a fragment of old web hung like a curtain. Tiny bones were tangled within it—too small to be human. Adanion caught the glint of fangs and thought better than to wonder what had made them.

'Someone—something—called this place home once,' he muttered.

'Hope they're long gone,' Kril replied, though without much conviction.

Suddenly, a thin wire snapped beneath Adanion's foot with a whispered, metallic ting.

'Trap,' Rhazha hissed, stepping back instantly and drawing her axe.

Adanion froze, eyes locking on the pair of rusted blades now swinging down from the ceiling. He ducked swiftly; the blades grazed his cloak, cold and razor-sharp.

'Nice reflexes,' Kril grunted approvingly.

Adanion smirked despite himself. 'Years of practice.'

They pressed onward, slower now, every step watched and measured, alert for any further dangers. The next chamber they entered was colder still, carved from smooth, polished stone.

Twin statues of orc warriors stood sentinel, their fierce faces cracked and weathered by time.
Kril gave one a cautious nudge. 'They look like they're about to jump us.'

Rhazha knelt to examine the floor carefully. 'Pressure plates. Step wrong, and those statues will come alive... or worse.'

The silence inside the chamber pressed against them, dense and expectant. It was the kind of quiet that lived in tombs—laden with the memory of violence. The statues didn't move, but their eyes, though blind with erosion, seemed to follow.

Adanion probed the floor's edges delicately with the tip of his sword.

'Hold,' Rhazha whispered suddenly. 'There's a tripwire

here.'

With steady hands, Adanion severed the wire cleanly.

'Good thing you have the steady hands,' Kril said, nodding with approval.

'They are indeed skilled,' Adanion replied, glancing at Rhazha with a grin.

Rhazha rolled her eyes. 'Keep moving, shivak.'

They crossed the chamber cautiously, each step deliberate and careful. As they moved deeper, the tunnels grew narrower, the air stale with the taste of dust and decay. A draft stirred now and then from below, carrying the scent of old stone and something... sweeter. Not rot, exactly—something perfumed, floral, long dead.

Adanion brushed dirt from his cloak and glanced at his companions. Kril hummed softly under his breath, a halfling dance tune from Mudwater that somehow eased the tension. Rhazha's axes caught the flickering torchlight, shimmering softly. She noticed Adanion watching her, measuring her movements as she shifted her grip on the blades.

She paused, voice low and fierce. 'My clan's motto was 'Strength in silence, fury in battle.' I carry that with me.'

Adanion nodded, respecting the quiet pride in her words. 'It suits you.'

The path narrowed further, walls bowing in like cracked ribs. They ducked beneath a fallen lintel, the stones scorched as if by lightning, though there was no soot. Ahead, a pale green glow licked the edges of an archway.

'Something's ahead,' Rhazha said.

'No turning back now,' Kril muttered.

Suddenly, the ground trembled beneath their feet. A sharp crack split the silence. The floor gave way beneath

Adanion's boots, and he plunged into darkness, tumbling down a narrow shaft. Dust swirled thinly as Kril and Rhazha scrambled to haul him from the pit's jaws.

The floor cracked and shifted again ominously.

'Careful,' Rhazha warned, eyes scanning the unstable ground. 'This place is crumbling.'

Adanion wiped blood from a split lip and grinned despite the pain. 'You could've let me die. I'm the charm.'

Kril rolled his eyes. 'Yeah, charm that gets us killed.'

Rhazha scowled but allowed a small smile. 'We're still alive. That counts.'

They pressed onward, stepping carefully past shattered pillars and pools of stagnant water. A ghostly, eerie glow illuminated a door carved with strange, twisting runes.

Adanion crouched to trace the symbols with a finger. 'Orcish and something older... protective wards,' he muttered.

Kril flexed his fingers on his axe. 'Let's get this over with.'

The door creaked open, revealing a chamber bathed in eerie, unnatural light. At its centre stood a stone dais. Resting atop it was the artefact—a heart-shaped crystal pulsing softly, like a heartbeat caught in stone.

Kril grunted. 'That's no ordinary relic.'

Rhazha didn't speak. She stared at the crystal in silence, her face unreadable. Her grip tightened on her axes.

Adanion glanced at her, then back at the artefact. 'You've seen this before?'

She hesitated just long enough. 'No.' The air thickened with the weight of the lie.

Kril stepped forward, axe raised. The artefact's glow deepened; shadows twisted unnaturally along the chamber walls. The sweet, dead perfume returned, laden in the air, as the artefact pulsed brighter.

'It's reacting,' Adanion said quietly. 'To us? Or just to being disturbed?'

Rhazha's voice was low, controlled. 'We need to be careful. It might be warded.'

The air thickened, oppressive with magic and menace. Kril positioned himself between the entrance and the dais, axe raised. The artefact's pulsing light intensified, casting shadows on the walls that twisted unnaturally, as if recoiling—or watching.

Rhazha's eyes narrowed. 'We're not alone.' A distant rumble echoed through the tunnels, the ground trembling beneath their feet once more.

'Ready?' Adanion asked, voice low but steady.

Rhazha nodded, axes raised, Kril grunted, muscles coiling like a spring.

Suddenly, the artefact's light blazed fiercely, bathing the chamber in a cold, unearthly glow. The air thickened, suffocating and syrupy, charged with ancient power that made the hairs on Kril's neck stand on end. From cracks in the walls, dark tendrils writhed like serpents—sinister and restless. The rumbling beneath their feet grew louder, shaking dust from the stones overhead.

Rhazha's grip on her axes whitened. 'Whatever's coming isn't natural,' she hissed, eyes darting to the tendrils that now slithered towards them, seeking flesh.

Adanion's blade gleamed as he stepped forward, positioning himself between the artefact and his companions. 'Stay close. Watch your flanks.'

Kril planted his massive feet firmly, axe raised like a battering ram. His breath came in slow, controlled bursts. 'Let's see what you've got.'

The tendrils lashed out—quick as vipers—snapping at

ankles and wrists. Kril swung his axe in a wide arc, the blade connecting with a hideous tendril, shredding it like paper. The smell of burnt flesh filled the chamber. Rhazha darted in, axes flashing, slicing clean through the creeping darkness. Her movements were brutal but precise, honed by years of battle. 'Don't let it touch you,' she warned, ducking under a sweeping lash.

Adanion weaved through the melee, sword striking with deadly precision. He moved with a grace that belied the danger, every slash pushing back the encroaching shadows. 'Keep the light on the artefact,' he commanded, voice steady.

Kril grunted and threw himself forward, blade cleaving through the nearest shade. 'Back off! It's ours!' he bellowed.

The artefact's rhythm stuttered—like a heart caught mid-beat—growing louder, faster, wrong. Rhazha shouted something, her voice swallowed by the vault's unravelling. Torchlight flickered wildly as dust filled the air, thick with the dry reek of stone and something sharp—like a snapped bone. Beneath it all, a low groan vibrated through the walls. The chamber shook violently. A fissure cracked open in the floor behind them, and from it emerged twisted, wraith-like horrors—creatures of shadow and bone, hollow eyes burning with malevolence.

'More of them!' Rhazha barked. 'Focus on the shadows!'

Adanion spun to face the new threat, deflecting a skeletal claw with the flat of his blade. Sparks flew from the impact. 'We need to hold this ground.'

The chamber rang with the clash of steel and the shriek of twisted magic. Shadows swirled like smoke given thought, pouring from the broken fissures in the walls and floor. They came in waves—twisting, half-formed things with too many limbs and eyes like dying coals. Each one that fell was replaced by two more. The pressure of it bore down like a storm.

Adanion stepped in close, one dagger drawn now alongside his sword, both dancing in a blur of silver. His movements were honed and fluid, a deadly rhythm that spoke of a lifetime spent turning elegance into violence. One shadow lunged with spined arms, jaws splitting impossibly wide. Adanion ducked low and spun, slicing through it in a fluid arc. Black mist sprayed as the creature unravelled. He didn't pause—another came from behind, but his dagger was already there, slipping between ribs that were no more than shadow.

Rhazha moved with him, axes spinning in tight arcs. Her strikes were not beautiful—just efficient. She cut through the shades with the precision of someone who'd never needed flair to kill. The fury in her movements matched the steel in her eyes, and she fought without fear, without pause. A tendril wrapped her arm—she snarled and ripped free, leaving a smear of blood on her bicep. One axe embedded in a shade's spine, while the other tore through its middle. Ash and bones scattered at her feet.

Kril roared again, holding the line near the dais. He was less dancer, more cyclone. Every swing of his axe tore through tendrils and shattered bone. When a wraith tried to leap past him, he caught it mid-air with a backhanded blow, sending it spiralling into the far wall where it shattered like pottery. A second beast dropped from the ceiling with a snarl. Kril didn't flinch. He ducked, rolled forward, then rose with a two-handed upward swing that split the thing clean in half. The pieces dissolved as they fell to the stone floor.

'Hold formation!' Adanion called. 'Don't get separated!'

The light from the artefact was pulsing faster now, too fast. It was like a heart nearing collapse—desperate, overstrained. The crystal flared with each blow struck, illuminating the horrors that stalked them from the edges. The shadows hated the light—they hissed, recoiled, then surged again with renewed frenzy. Magic screamed in the air. Sparks burst where blade met bone, and the stone beneath their feet was slick with ichor.

One of the wraiths let out a piercing cry, a sound that clawed straight into the bones. Rhazha staggered, clutching her head, but Kril grabbed her collar and yanked her back before a tendril could snare her ankle.

'Thanks,' she growled, recovering her stance.

'Buy me a drink later,' Kril muttered, swinging again.

Adanion reached the dais, blades slick with dark ichor, sweat trickling down his temple as he stared at the crystal. The artefact pulsed softly now, vibrating on the stone like it was trying to break free.

'I think it's drawing them,' he said through gritted teeth. 'They're protecting it—or bound to it.'

'So smash it,' Kril barked, swinging through a wraith.

'No!' Adanion snapped. 'Break the link, not the artefact. It's too powerful—we'd unleash gods-know-what.'

He ducked beneath a slashing claw, twisted, and drove his dagger into the creature's side. It shrieked and dissipated in a burst of black mist.

'We need to sever the connection—disrupt the anchor, not destroy it.'

'And how do we do that?' Rhazha shouted, blocking two tendrils with her crossed axes.

They were boxed in now, the circle tightening. Wraiths climbed the broken walls, crawling like insects, heads twitching, jaws gnashing. Rhazha cleaved one in two as it leapt, then swept both axes in a wide arc to clear space for Adanion.

Adanion didn't answer at once. His mind was racing, every sense flooded with heat and cold and sound. He reached inside his cloak with one hand, pulling out a small satchel of powder—ground silver, chalk, and dried clover.

'Circle of Severance,' he muttered. 'Get me some space!'

Kril and Rhazha covered him without hesitation. While they fought, Adanion began to draw a quick, tight circle around the base of the dais, scattering the powder with practised hands. The air sparked where it fell, hissing as the components met the ancient magic saturating the floor.

He'd used it once before. It had worked. Mostly.

Rhazha snarled as a claw raked her arm. She drove a boot into the creature's chest and hacked it down with a roar.

'Hope your witchcraft works fast, shivak!'

'Come on, come on...' he breathed, finishing the last arc of the circle.

As he completed the mark, the ground shook with a deep, throbbing hum. The glow of the artefact flared one final time, and then dimmed. Not extinguished—but quieted.

The wraiths screamed, flailing and writhing as the link was broken. One by one, they began to fall apart and dissolve, collapsing into piles of dust and bone. In moments, the chamber was still again.

Adanion straightened, sweat gleaming on his brow, breath shallow. 'That should buy us time. Maybe days. Maybe minutes.'

Kril kicked one of the withered remains. 'Long enough to get the damned thing out of here?'

Adanion looked at the artefact, now quiet in the eerie hush. 'Long enough to move it safely. But we'll want a containment field. And wards. Lots of them.'

Rhazha leaned on one axe, brushing dust from her brow. 'Let's not stick around long enough to find out what round two looks like.'

'Agreed,' Kril said, wrapping the crystal gingerly with a massive, rune-etched material from Adanion's pack.

As they turned back towards the corridor, the air behind them stirred again—just a whisper this time. A reminder that the Bonecrack Ruins had not given up all their secrets. And that some things, once disturbed, are never truly still. The chamber trembled again, cracks racing along the ceiling. A slab of stone crashed behind them, smashing the dais in half.

'Time's up,' Rhazha said, urgency flaring in her voice.

Adanion didn't wait. 'Move!'

They sprinted for the entrance, the ground buckling beneath them. More stones rained from above. The corridor behind them collapsed in waves, swallowing the chamber whole. Torchlight flickered wildly as dust filled the air. The deafening roar of stone grinding on stone chased them.

At the entrance, Kril grabbed the edge and hauled himself out. Rhazha followed, pulling Adanion from the darkness below. They tumbled onto the mossy earth outside the ruin—alive, breathless, covered in dust and sweat.

For a moment, nothing moved. The forest waited—still and dark. Cool air pressed against their skin, carrying the scent of pine and soil. Somewhere above, a bird called once and fell silent. Starlight shimmered through the branches. They lay still, breathing hard, while above them, the stars burned cold and bright.

Kril turned. No wraiths followed.

Behind them, the ruins groaned—one last, deep sigh—before a final roar of collapsing stone sealed the entrance forever.

'Well,' said Kril, panting, 'that was unpleasant. I hate ruins.'

Adanion caught his breath. 'What did we learn?'

Kril leaned on his axe. 'Don't touch glowy crystals?'

'Correct.'

The trio stayed where they'd fallen—chests heaving, hearts pounding. The artefact's eerie glow faded from memory, replaced by the sharp bite of relief. Adanion dragged a sleeve across his face, voice hoarse but triumphant. 'We didn't come for an easy score.'

Rhazha's gaze lingered on the ruins, sadness flickering in her eyes. 'The Bonecrack Ruins hold their secrets tight... and their regrets.'

Kril grunted, a rare grin breaking through. 'We're still standing. That's gotta count for something.'

Above, the night sky stretched cold and distant. Adanion sheathed his sword. 'Tomorrow, we plan our next move. But tonight... we rest.'

Rhazha winced as she sat up. 'Next time, we bring more torches.'

Kril spat, then smirked. 'Bring all the torches you want. I'll still want ale after.'

Their laughter, rough and raw, echoed softly as they settled in under the stars, warriors united by danger and resolve.

CHAPTER NINE

ORCISH HOSPITALITY INVOLVES SCREAMING

T HEY EMERGED FROM THE SUFFOCATING darkness of the twisting tunnels into a cavernous space that must have once been a grand feasting hall. Now, it was a brutal war camp, scarred and reeking of sweat, smoke, and the harsh tang of stale ale. The walls, once carved with intricate tribal motifs, were marred with crude banners and the blood-red tusks of the Iron Tusks warband. Rough-hewn wooden tables were overturned or repurposed as makeshift barricades. The flickering light of smoky braziers cast shadows that danced like savage spirits along the blackened stone.

Adanion's boots crunched over the uneven floor, strewn with splinters, bones, and discarded weapons. A knot tightened in his stomach. He glanced sideways at Rhazha, who was every inch a shadow blending with the murky gloom—silent, tense, a predator in her element, yet bound by danger. He wondered what she saw in this place that he couldn't, what ancient memories or fresh scars this cavern held for her.

Rhazha inhaled sharply, nostrils flaring. The air was a cacophony of smells, each one a different kind of threat. 'Stay close,' she warned in a low voice. 'They don't know I betrayed them yet.'

'Yet?' Kril's voice was a low rumble, heavy with curiosity and a touch of sarcasm.

Rhazha's eyes flickered to him, a shadow crossing her face. 'Long story,' she said tightly. 'Involving fire. And a certain chieftain's daughter.'

Adanion raised an eyebrow, intrigued. He was used to the blunt, practical truths of life on the road, but Rhazha's past was a landscape of mystery and broken loyalties he was just beginning to explore. 'You're full of surprises.'

She shot him a grim smile. 'Try to keep up.'

The three moved forward with caution, weaving between clusters of burly orcs who bellowed crude war chants or drank deeply from horned mugs. Every shadow seemed alive, every grunt and scrape a potential threat. The stench of sweat and stale meat was overwhelming—an assault on the senses that made Adanion's skin prickle. He felt a bead of sweat trickle down his spine, unrelated to the heat from the braziers. It was the simple, animal fear of being surrounded by a hundred things that wanted to kill him.

They had rehearsed their story until it felt almost believable: mercenaries hired to deliver a special prisoner to the Iron Tusks. Kril bore heavy, fake chains rattling with each step, the clinking noise oddly satisfying. Adanion played the watchful guard, his sword resting lightly in its sheath but ready. Rhazha kept her expression carefully neutral, eyes sharp and alert.

For a moment, the ruse held. Several orcs stared with suspicion, but the warband's eyes were elsewhere, drunk on the frenzy of their preparations for an upcoming raid. The prisoners and spoils of war were routine.

Then a voice—a rough, guttural bark—cut through the din like a blade.

'VRAK'THAK ZHURUK!'
(That's the traitor!)

The cavern fell instantly silent, the tension snapping taut as fifteen orcs drew weapons in unison. Iron-shod boots thundered across the floorboards as more orcs gathered, faces twisted in rage. One orc, massive and scarred, blew a horn with a shrill, grating blast that echoed through the chamber. It was a call to arms—a summons to violent retribution.

Kril sighed with something close to relief. 'Finally.'

Without hesitation, he ripped off the fake chains, muscles bunching as he hefted his axe. The gleam in his eye was unbridled and savage, the battle lust of a seasoned warrior unleashed.

Adanion's mind went blank, all thought subsumed by instinct. He ducked low just as a brutal axe came crashing down where his head had been seconds before. The whoosh of displaced air was a violent whisper. He rolled across an overturned table, the wood splintering under his weight, then sprang up and sliced through an orc's forearm with a clean, sharp stroke. Blood spattered across his face, hot and coppery.

'Why do you always swing first?' Adanion shouted over the clash of steel.

'Because it works!' Kril bellowed back, grinning through the mayhem as he swung his axe in a devastating arc.

Rhazha was already halfway up a scaffold, axes spinning with deadly precision. Her movements were fluid, almost elegant in their brutality. 'Get to the artefact vault! I'll cover you. Go!'

Adanion shoved a heavy table across the floor, creating a

barrier between himself and the advancing horde. Ducking behind it, he muttered, 'Right then. To the vault it is.'

The battle was a fever dream of blood and steel. Orcs roared like wild beasts, hacking and slashing with crude, savage weapons. The air was thick with the metallic scent of blood and the acrid smoke from burning torches. Adanion could feel every heartbeat pounding in his ears, every breath burning in his lungs as adrenaline surged.

Kril smashed through a line of attackers with relentless fury, his axe cleaving bone and sinew alike. Even he was pushed back, forced to retreat towards the labyrinthine passages leading deeper into the ruin.

Adanion parried a vicious swing and countered with a quick slash, driving his opponent back. The force of the blow rattled his arm. He noted with grim satisfaction that his form was holding, even under pressure. The flicker of torchlight revealed the orc's snarling, tusked face—so close, so brutal.

From above, Rhazha's voice rang clear, cutting through the turmoil. 'Move faster! The vault is just ahead!'

Adanion sprinted, dodging overturned crates and fallen warriors, the pounding of Orcish footsteps close behind. The weight of the situation pressed on him: the artefact had to be secured, or all their efforts would be for naught.

Rhazha leapt down from the scaffold just as Kril arrived, and the three converged at a heavy iron door—its surface etched with ancient runes and chipped from centuries of neglect. Adanion produced a set of lock picks from his belt, his fingers steady despite the pounding in his chest. 'This better be the right door.'

Kril crouched beside him, axe raised defensively. Rhazha scanned the room, eyes sharp for any sign of ambush.

A faint grinding sound echoed as the lock yielded, and the heavy door creaked open, revealing a chamber bathed in cold, eerie light. The air inside was thick with magic, heavy and almost suffocating. The cold pricked at Adanion's skin, a chilling contrast to the heat of the battle they had just left.

At the centre, resting on a stone pedestal, was the artefact—gleaming with an otherworldly glow, its facets pulsing like a heartbeat.

Rhazha's eyes narrowed as she stepped forward. 'There it is.'

Adanion reached out, his heart racing, but as his fingers brushed the artefact's surface, a sudden, violent tremor shook the chamber. Dust fell from the ceiling, and the shadows deepened. Outside, the war cries of orcs grew louder—a reminder that their time was running out.

'Grab it!' Rhazha snapped.

Adanion wrapped his hands around the artefact, feeling a pulse of energy surge through him, raw and wild. It felt like holding a caged storm, dangerous and unpredictable.

Kril hefted the door shut just as the first orcs burst into the chamber, weapons raised and snarling. The three braced themselves, backs to the stone wall, ready to face the storm. The orcs slammed against the heavy iron door, their brutal fists pounding like thunder, the sound vibrating through the very stones beneath their feet. Kril planted his feet, straining to hold it shut, sweat beading along his brow, mingling with the dust and grime of the hall.

'We can't hold them forever,' Adanion said, his voice low and steady despite the storm battering the door.

Rhazha's eyes darted between the heavy wooden beams and the narrow stairwell leading upward. 'There's a second exit,' she said, her voice clipped with urgency. 'A servant's passage. We take that and disappear before they regroup.'

Kril grunted, muscles taut. 'Sounds like a plan, if we survive this.'

A massive orc rammed the door with the full weight of his bulk, and it groaned, shifting dangerously. Kril slammed his shoulder into the door, the muscle tautening on his back, forcing it closed. 'We don't have time for hesitation.'

Adanion caught Rhazha's eye, and in that brief glance passed a silent command: no heroics, no distractions—just get the artefact and get out alive.

Rhazha nodded, her axes gleaming in the eerie glow of the chamber's magic. 'Cover me. I'm going first.'

Adanion's eyes flicked down, then up at her. He muttered, 'I hate when you say things like that.'

'Because it means we're doing something stupid?' Kril asked, wiping sweat and blood from his brow.

'Exactly.'

Kril released one last grunt, then pivoted to face the crowd gathering beyond the heavy door, ready to meet them. 'I'll buy you some time.'

Adanion glanced around, noting the narrowness of the servant's passage—too tight for all three to flee at once. 'We split up here,' he said. 'Rhazha and I take the passage. Kril holds the hall.'

'No way,' Kril growled, stepping closer. 'I'm not dying in some corner while you two sneak off an leave me for dead.'

Adanion held up a hand, calm but firm. 'It's not about dying—it's about surviving. We'll need you alive if we want to fight another day.'

Rhazha cut in sharply, 'We don't have a day. We have minutes, if that.'

The orc horn sounded again, louder and more frantic, echoing through the stone corridors. The Iron Tusks were regrouping—getting their act together.

Kril's shoulders slumped. 'Fine. But if I'm last out, you better be ready to carry me.'

Adanion cracked a rare smile. 'Deal.'

Kril slammed his shoulder against the door one last time, then pivoted, gripping his axe tightly as the warband burst into the chamber. 'Get going! I'll catch up with you at the rendezvous!'

Rhazha moved like a shadow, already slipping into the narrow passageway. Adanion followed close, sword drawn, his senses on fire with anticipation and danger. The passage was a tight squeeze, damp and stifling, the walls slick with moss and grime. Every step echoed faintly, and the faint sounds of Orcish curses and battle cries receded behind them. Suddenly, a faint clicking noise sounded—a trap. Rhazha froze, scanning the floor with sharp eyes.

'Pressure plate,' she hissed. 'Step wrong, and it'll trigger a volley of arrows.'

Adanion's eyes flicked down, spotting the telltale pattern of small holes in the ceiling and narrow slits in the walls.

'We move slow,' he said. 'One at a time.'

Carefully, painfully, they made their way through the trap-laden corridor, hearts pounding not just from the fight but from the deadly precision required.

While Adanion and Rhazha made their careful way through the tunnels, back in the great hall, Kril had taken a stand at the heart of the warband's encampment. He wielded his axe with brutal efficiency, swinging wide and striking true. Orcs fell around him, but more surged forward like a tide, fierce and unyielding. Ragged gasps tore from him as he fought for survival—and for his friends' chance to escape with the artefact. Every blow was fuelled by rage and desperation, every parry a fight against overwhelming odds.

A massive orc stepped forward, towering over the others and dragging a spiked mace the size of a log. Scars lined his arms and chest—trophies of countless battles—and he sneered at Kril with bloodlust in his eyes. With a roar, he charged. The ground shook as the two collided—mace swinging in brutal arcs, Kril ducking low and twisting away with a predator's grace. Sparks flew where steel kissed stone, and the air filled with the reek of sweat and iron. Kril moved like a storm contained, each strike of his axe deliberate, each dodge tauntingly close.

'You fight like a demon!' the orc growled.

'Demon?' Kril bared his teeth. 'I'm holding back.'

He slammed the flat of his axe into the orc's knee with a sickening crack. The brute buckled with a howl, collapsing onto one leg—his weapon falling wide. Kril didn't finish him. He didn't need to. He stepped past the fallen warrior like he was nothing more than a dropped shield. Silence rippled through the others. Not fear. Not yet. But something colder: awareness.

Back in the corridor, Adanion and Rhazha finally emerged into a smaller, dimly lit chamber. Here, the air felt thicker with magic, ancient and brooding. The walls were lined with dusty crates and broken relics—forgotten spoils of countless raids and wars. Rhazha moved to the far corner, where a faint blue glow shimmered beneath a cracked stone slab.

'There,' she whispered.

Adanion knelt beside her, examining the slab and the faint runes glowing softly at its edges. 'Ready for another round?' he asked, his voice low.

Rhazha nodded, axes at the ready. 'Let's finish this.'

Together, they lifted the slab, revealing a small alcove

beneath—a hidden cache. Inside rested a second artefact, smaller but no less potent: a dark crystal pulsing with ominous energy. Adanion's fingers trembled as he reached out, but Rhazha's hand caught his wrist.

'Wait,' she said. 'There's a ward. If we touch it wrong, it'll alert the entire fortress.'

Adanion frowned. 'Great.'

Rhazha stepped back, drawing a small dagger etched with ancient symbols from her belt. 'Give me a moment.' Her hands moved deftly, tracing the runes with precision. The ward hissed faintly, then faded. She carefully lifted the crystal, the weight of it both physical and metaphorical.

'Got it,' she said.

Adanion looked from the dark crystal in her hand to the direction they had come. 'Two relics now. One pulses with life, this one with death. Are you going to tell us what these things are for?'

Rhazha tucked the dark crystal securely into a belt pouch, keeping it separate from the first artefact. 'It's classified,' she murmured, her voice flat. 'They're part of the payment. The client will tell us if we need to know.'

Just then, a shout echoed down the corridor—a warning. Rhazha's brow furrowed. 'They're coming.'

Rhazha and Adanion exchanged a glance, a silent agreement passing between them. 'Time to disappear.'

Back in the main hall, Kril fought his way towards the servant's exit. Orcs blocked his path, snarling and swinging their weapons. With a roar, Kril pushed through, his axe swinging in deadly arcs. His muscles screamed, his vision blurred with sweat and blood. A massive orc blocked the exit, snarling with rage. Kril met him head-on, axe against axe, the sound ringing like thunder. For a moment, neither gave ground. Then, with a savage grin, Kril feinted left and drove his axe into the orc's side, sending him crashing to the floor. Breathing heavily, Kril staggered through the exit, collapsing just inside the passage. The narrow corridor swallowed him into darkness.

Adanion and Rhazha were already moving fast, the crystal and artefact secured. The tunnels twisted and turned, a labyrinth designed to trap intruders. Orcish shouts echoed behind them, closer now. Rhazha glanced over her shoulder. 'Almost there.'

Adanion's sword was ready in his hand, muscles coiled like springs. They burst into a wider chamber—a forgotten armoury littered with rusted weapons and shattered shields. 'This way!' Rhazha urged, sprinting towards a narrow stairwell spiralling upward. They ascended quickly, the sounds of pursuit growing distant but no less threatening. At the top, a heavy wooden door creaked open onto a steep hillside bathed in moonlight.

Freedom.

But before they could catch their breath, a guttural growl rumbled behind them. A hulking orc barred their path, eyes blazing with fury and betrayal. Rhazha stepped forward, axes gleaming. 'This ends now.'

Rhazha's axes gleamed in the moonlight as she squared off against the hulking orc. His snarling face was twisted with rage, the scars of countless battles etched deep into his green skin. He wielded a massive, crude hammer, its head studded with jagged iron spikes.

Adanion stood beside her, his blade drawn, his eyes narrowing with fierce determination. 'Hold your ground,' he said, his voice low but commanding.

The orc charged, a thunderous crash shaking the ground beneath their feet. Rhazha met him head-on, spinning with savage grace as her axes arced through the air, aiming to find the gaps in his brutal defence. The hammer slammed down with bone-crushing force, but Rhazha twisted away just in time, the weapon smashing into the stone where she had stood moments before.

Adanion lunged forward, his sword flashing in a deadly arc, forcing the orc to stagger back. The beast roared and swung wildly, reckless and furious. Rhazha seized the opening and drove one axe deep into his thigh. The orc bellowed in pain, collapsing onto one knee but still fighting. Adanion pressed forward, his steel biting into flesh as he struck again and again, relentless.

Finally, the orc's resistance faltered. With a final cry, he fell face-first into the dirt, motionless.

Rhazha wiped sweat from her brow, breathing hard. 'That was too close.'

Adanion nodded, sheathing his sword. 'We don't have much time.' He glanced back down the winding path. 'If Kril's alive, he's making his way to the rendezvous. We just have to survive until then.'

From below came the faint, distant clash of steel—the unmistakable sounds of battle still raging. Rhazha looked at the darkened forest beyond the hillside. 'We need to disappear into the trees.'

Rhazha hefted the crystal carefully. 'Let's move.'

The moonlit forest was a maze of shadows and whispering leaves. They moved quickly, careful not to make noise, every snap of a twig a threat. Behind them, the fortress glowed faintly—a grim reminder of the war they had escaped but had not yet won. Suddenly, a figure stepped from the shadows ahead.

Kril.

Bloodied, bruised, but alive.

'About time,' Rhazha said with a grim smile.

Kril grunted, his breath ragged. 'I told you I'd make it.'

Adanion clapped him on the shoulder. 'Good. We have what we came for.'

The three exchanged a look—united, battle-worn, but unbroken. Their journey was far from over. The forest air was thick with damp earth and the scent of pine, mingled with the faint metallic tang of blood still fresh on their skin and clothes. Every snap of a twig beneath their boots seemed deafening in the stillness, every rustle of leaves a whispered warning that danger lurked just beyond sight.

Kril limped slightly, favouring one leg, but he pushed on with grim determination. 'We can't afford to rest—not yet.'

Rhazha kept close, her dual axes strapped to her back now, hands free but ready. 'The Iron Tusks won't follow us into these woods. They're brutes, not trackers.'

Adanion's gaze scanned the dark underbrush, his eyes sharp as a hawk's. 'That may be so, but we can't underestimate them. Orcs are clever when cornered—and desperate.'

A sudden crack echoed behind them. All three froze, muscles coiled like springs. Rhazha spun, her hand on her axe, but only a shadow darted between the trees.

'False alarm,' Kril said, though his voice carried the edge of doubt.

The path ahead narrowed, a tangled thicket that forced them to move single file. Rhazha went first, her knife slicing through thorny branches that scraped her skin, leaving shallow scratches.

'Why'd you bring us this way?' Adanion muttered, wincing as a branch caught the back of his neck.

'Because the old roads are watched,' Rhazha said without

looking back. 'This way, we lose the trail.'

Kril swallowed hard, grimacing. 'And what then? We walk for days? Starve?'

'We'll find shelter,' Rhazha replied, her eyes fierce. 'We survive, or we die trying.'

Their breath rose in clouds, mingling with the mist curling low between the trees. The moon was a sliver above, casting faint silver light through the canopy. The forest felt alive—watching, waiting.

A rustle to their left—a pair of glowing eyes.

Adanion dropped to one knee, his hand on the hilt of his sword. 'Wolves.'

Rhazha's gaze narrowed. 'Hungry ones. Stay calm.'

The pack emerged, silent as shadows—lean, hungry beasts with fur mottled like the forest floor. Their eyes gleamed, teeth bared in low growls.

Kril stepped forward, his axe raised. 'I don't want to fight you.'

The alpha wolf snarled, inching closer.

Rhazha's hand went to the hilt of her dagger. 'Back off, or we'll have no choice.'

Tension crackled in the cold air. Then, as if deciding the intruders weren't worth the trouble, the wolves melted back into the shadows, vanishing as suddenly as they appeared.

Kril exhaled slowly. 'That was too close.'

They pressed onward, silence falling again. Hours passed in a blur of stumbling footsteps, whispered plans, and aching limbs. The forest thinned into rolling hills bathed in predawn light. Rhazha pointed towards a cluster of weathered stone ruins half-swallowed by vines. 'There. Shelter.'

They hurried towards the remnants of a crumbled watchtower, its walls cracked but still standing enough to shield them. Inside, they collapsed, catching their breath. Adanion carefully inspected the crystal, turning it over in his hands. 'We're lucky to have it.'

Kril nodded, rubbing his bruised shoulder. 'Luck and skill.'

Rhazha looked out a broken window, her eyes narrowing. 'Luck won't save us next time. We need a plan—and allies.'

Silence settled as they considered the long road ahead—one paved with danger, sacrifice, and uncertain hope. But for now, in the quiet ruin beneath the rising sun, they found a brief moment to rest.

CHAPTER TEN

VAULT BREAK-IN & EMOTIONAL TURMOIL (SORT OF)

THEY FOUGHT THEIR WAY THROUGH a maze of broken pillars and scattered crates, the orcs in relentless pursuit. Rhazha darted ahead, her breath ragged but steady, leading them through a narrow service corridor that twisted beneath the hall.

The sounds of combat ricocheted through the stone halls—shouted commands, the clang of steel on steel, the guttural snarls of wounded orcs. Each step sent splinters of pain up their legs, not from wounds, but from pure exertion. Rubble crunched beneath their boots, the torchlight flickering behind them as scattered flames from a toppled brazier licked at the broken walls. Somewhere behind, an orc bellowed something in their brutal, growling tongue—and the echoes seemed to chase them like wolves on the hunt.

'Almost there,' she gasped.

She didn't look back. She didn't need to. She could feel the heat of pursuit, the tremble of heavy feet pounding after them. With a sharp twist, she pressed her palm against the wall as they rounded another bend, barely keeping herself upright. Every corner brought new danger—more debris, collapsed archways, twisted remnants of a once-great stronghold. It was a maze of memory and decay, but she had walked these paths in dreams since she was old enough to wield a dagger.

The echoes of war cries and clashing steel grew fainter as the trio slipped deeper into the fortress's guts. A sudden hush settled over them as they came into a narrow chamber where the dust hung so thick it veiled the torchlight. The air was still here—dead still. Even the sounds of pursuit had dulled, as if the fortress itself were holding its breath. A collapsed arch lay to one side, its stones cracked like bones, and above it, half-shadowed, was the mark: a curling firebrand crest.

The vault door loomed before them—massive, ancient, and scarred with the weight of centuries. It was carved from a single slab of obsidian-black stone, its surface etched with the jagged, curling markings of what Adanion assumed was a long-dead clan, worn but unmistakable. Adanion's gaze tracked the jagged design. 'A crest,' he murmured, his voice low and tight. He glanced at Rhazha, whose eyes were fixed on to the stone. 'Whatever they kept here, they clearly wanted it to stay kept.'

Faint traces of dust and rusted iron clung to the door frame, whispering of decades, perhaps centuries, of forgotten history. The space before the door was quiet, save for the three of them breathing hard. Even the fortress seemed to fall reverently silent in the presence of this relic.

'This has to be it,' Rhazha said, her voice low. She didn't look at Adanion, nor acknowledge his observation.

She stepped closer, brushing her fingertips against the carving. A tremor passed through her—not from the cold, but from recognition. She hadn't been born in this fortress, hadn't seen these markings with her own eyes. But stories had blood, and hers ran thick with Emberfang.

Kril nodded, dropping into a crouch by the lock. 'Now what?'

The flicker of urgency returned to their movements. From behind them came a distant echo—faint, but certain. Their time was bleeding away.

Adanion pulled out a thin silver pick, the faintest smile tugging at the corner of his mouth. 'Watch and learn.'

Rhazha raised a brow, still catching her breath as she studied the vault. 'You're telling me you can pick that?'

Adanion smirked, an edge of confident arrogance shining through the dust and grime on his face. 'I've picked worse.'

Kril crouched beside him, already scanning the corridor behind them for movement. 'He says that every time,' he muttered, a touch of dry amusement in his voice. He didn't bother watching Adanion work—he knew how this part went. Instead, he flicked a glance towards Rhazha, who stood a pace behind them, her shoulder resting against the wall. Her breathing had steadied, but her eyes were locked on the door, the weight of what lay beyond pressing down on her like a mountain.

She wasn't afraid. Not exactly. But something about this place felt... old in a way no ruins should. Like the walls themselves remembered, and disliked being disturbed.

Adanion set to work, fingers nimble and sure despite the chill in the air. The lock resisted—ancient magic seemed woven with the mechanical tumblers, but the pick slid and clicked with practised precision.

Seconds stretched. A breath held.

Then—click.

The vault door groaned, an ancient sound that echoed like a warning through the corridors. It slowly swung open, revealing the dim interior beyond. A stale gust of air breathed out from the chamber, thick with dust and the dry, metallic scent of time. The hinges shrieked as the door shifted further, reluctant to release whatever secrets it had guarded for so long. A low vibration hummed through the floor beneath their boots—subtle, but enough to raise the hairs on their arms. Magic still clung to the chamber like a ghost refusing to leave.

No one spoke for a moment.

The light from their torch spilt across the threshold, revealing a long, narrow chamber lined with shelves. Shadows stretched along the walls like reaching hands, broken by the jagged shapes of stored relics. The shelves, once neatly arranged, now sagged under the weight of forgotten treasures and ruin. Cracked urns and dust-covered scrolls lined the walls—gilded trinkets and weaponry dulled by time. A great iron standard leaned against one wall, its banner half-shredded, the Emberfang insignia barely visible through the grime. A pair of ancient boots sat beneath it, petrified by time. Each relic was a story, each one a fragment of a people long gone.

They stepped cautiously inside, the air heavy with stillness. Rhazha went first, her hand trailing along the stone wall as though needing the contact to steady herself. Her boots crunched softly over grit and broken tile. There was reverence in her movements—not fear, but a solemnity that made Kril slow his own steps in response.

Even Adanion, usually brash in his movements, moved with measured care. His gaze swept over the collection with an appraiser's eye, but there was no smug comment this time. Just silence.

But there, resting on a pedestal carved from black stone,

was the artefact: a single obsidian blade, glowing faintly with dark red runes that pulsed in rhythm with some unseen heartbeat.

The pedestal stood in the chamber's centre like an altar, raised slightly above the floor, the stone around it cracked in a near-perfect circle—as if the magic within the blade had reshaped the earth itself to make room. Dust didn't seem to cling to it like the others. The area around it was eerily clean, as though the blade repelled decay. The sword was shorter than expected—almost delicate in shape—but that only made it more unsettling. Its edges curved like a serpent's fang, and the runes embedded into the obsidian surface bled with a dull, rhythmic glow. The light was not constant. It pulsed—softly, steadily—like a slow heartbeat. Like something alive.

The red light reflected in Rhazha's eyes as she stepped closer. Her breath caught. It had a presence. Not just a weapon. Something more. As if it were watching them, or perhaps dreaming and about to wake.

Rhazha's voice was barely a whisper, hoarse and urgent. 'That's it. The Emberfang.'

She stared at it, transfixed. For a heartbeat, she didn't move—just stood there, rooted to the ground, her eyes drinking in the weapon that had been ripped from her grasp. She had last seen it smeared with blood, but they had not prepared her for the peace of its presence here. The blade's aura was not just power—it was tangible regret, pressing against her skin like a physical presence. This was not a myth. It was a betrayal she had carried.

Adanion stepped forward, eyes fixed on the blade as if it were alive. He reached out, fingers curling around the hilt. The runes flared brighter, a cold pulse thrumming through the air. His breath hitched—not from effort, but something else. A sharp, unnatural chill slid up his arm, then down his spine. His fingers tightened around the hilt. It was like gripping ice that pulsed with fire underneath.

'This thing feels cursed,' he said, his voice low and uneasy.

Rhazha's gaze didn't waver. 'It probably is. But it belongs to my clan.'

She stepped forward slowly, almost reverently, until she stood beside Adanion. Her eyes dropped to the sword in his hand, its glow casting faint crimson light over their faces. She could feel it calling to her. It wasn't a voice. Not really. Just a pressure—a pull in her chest like gravity, like blood recognising blood. The weight of her words hung heavy. This wasn't just a weapon—they were holding the legacy of a people in their hands. A legacy soaked in betrayal and flame.

She reached for the hilt, and Adanion let her take it without resistance. The moment her fingers closed around it, something shifted in the chamber. A breathless hush. Like the room itself was watching. The blade seemed to drink in the dim light, the dark runes bleeding shadows that stretched along the stone floor like creeping fingers.

A cold sweat formed on Rhazha's brow, but she didn't release it. The hilt was oddly warm now—almost welcoming. It fit her grip too perfectly, as though shaped for her hand alone. The crimson runes pulsed once more, brighter this time, and the faint whisper of power curled through her veins.

Behind her, Adanion stepped back cautiously. He didn't say anything, but his hand hovered near his belt, ready for whatever happened next.

Kril watched from the edge of the chamber, brow furrowed. He hadn't said a word since they entered. There was something in his expression—not suspicion exactly, but wariness. He didn't like magic. Never had. And the kind of magic that left shadows crawling across the floor like living things? That was the worst kind. Still, he didn't move. Not yet.

Rhazha exhaled slowly, forcing herself to blink. To focus.

'It remembers,' she murmured, unsure if she was speaking aloud or thinking too loudly.

Kril shifted uneasily, eyes darting towards the hallway.

'Question,' Kril said, voice sharp with caution. 'How many orcs does it take to make that much noise?'

Before anyone could answer, the echoing war cry shattered the silence like a thunderclap, rattling the walls, and then—

Twenty.

A savage roar erupted behind them, and the heavy footsteps of orcs thundered down the corridor. Their snarls grew louder, a tidal wave of brutal fury breaking loose. The walls trembled. Dust sifted from the ceiling. Somewhere deeper in the fortress, a stone beam cracked with a groan. The ancient vault had held its breath for centuries, but now it woke to ruin.

Adanion spun, dropping the blade carefully onto the pedestal. 'We're out of time!'

Even as he turned, the glow from the Emberfang blade flickered once—like a warning or a protest—and then steadied. Rhazha's hand hovered for half a heartbeat over the hilt before she yanked it back into her grip. Whatever connection she'd felt, whatever hesitation lingered, vanished in the face of what was coming.

The thunder of orc boots grew louder. Close. No more than a dozen paces out now. Kril didn't wait—he was already tearing the rusted chains from his wrists, their clang lost in the building noise of pursuit. They fell to the stone floor with a dull thud, just as he sprinted towards the exit. Adanion gave the pedestal one final glance, as if memorising the blade's resting place, then turned and ran.

Rhazha hesitated for just a breath. The vault's air still clung to her skin—heavy, charged. She looked back once at the walls lined with relics, with memory. This was what remained of her people. Dust and ruin. A sword no one should have had to carry. And now—

Now it was hers.

She gritted her teeth, adjusted her grip on the Emberfang, and dashed after the others.

Kril yanked the fake chains from his wrists and sprinted towards the exit, the clatter of his bare feet sounding reckless but determined. The chains hit the ground with a heavy clang that echoed after him. His muscles screamed in protest—he'd taken a javelin graze earlier and it was starting to burn—but there was no time to slow down. Behind them, the orcs' pursuit surged forward with renewed fury, boots pounding like war drums. Rhazha grabbed the Emberfang blade again, feeling the pulse of its dark power through her veins as she dashed after him.

The vault's cool air gave way to the searing heat of adrenaline. The corridor ahead was narrow and uneven, with rubble scattered from long-forgotten battles and structural collapse. Rhazha's breath came sharp and fast, her eyes scanning for movement ahead even as her grip on the blade tightened. It responded—she could feel it. Like the weapon wanted blood.

Adanion fell in just behind her, pivoting mid-run to send a dagger spinning over her shoulder. A shriek rang out—an orc had rounded the corner too soon. The blade buried itself in the creature's throat, and it crashed backwards into the darkness. Another came right behind it.

'Move!' he barked. 'Don't slow down!'

Arrows hissed past, some grazing their arms, others

thudding into the walls or shattering the stone floor. Javelins flew in deadly arcs, missing by inches, their whistling screams filling the narrow passage. The sound was deafening. Wind sliced past their ears with each near-miss, and stone dust burst from the walls where the projectiles struck. One arrow ripped through Rhazha's sleeve, just nicking the skin beneath. She didn't falter—barely flinched—but her grip on the Emberfang tightened further, as if the weapon had felt the blood and approved.

'Split up!' Adanion yelled, diving behind a fallen pillar for cover.

Stone splintered around him as two arrows struck the top of the column, sending shards raining down like hail. He crouched low, drew another dagger, and peered around the edge. The corridor swam with movement—shadows and snarls and flame-lit figures in pursuit. He could make out at least a dozen orcs closing in fast, more crowding behind.

Rhazha didn't hesitate. She sprinted for the side door, lungs burning, muscles screaming. The door was half-rotted, cracked down the centre, but it gave way under her shoulder with a groan. She stumbled into the adjoining passage, heart hammering. Behind her, the sounds of pursuit thickened—gravel crunching under booted feet, the ragged roar of orc breath. And then—

Behind her, a hand grabbed her shoulder—an orc, eyes wild, teeth bared. Its grip was iron. She barely had time to twist free, instinct overriding thought. She turned fast, swinging the Emberfang blade in a wide arc. The dark runes flared as the blade cut through the air and sank deep into the orc's shoulder. The impact jarred up her arm like striking stone, but the result was immediate. The orc's body seized, a violent shudder running through its frame as the runes pulsed brighter, feeding on something unseen.

The creature roared in pain but lunged again. It didn't seem to care about the wound. Its arm hung limp at its side, blood pouring freely, but it still came at her with a low, gurgling snarl. Rhazha gritted her teeth, swinging again. The glow of the blade seemed to intensify with each strike, as if feeding on the orc's fury. The next blow caught the orc's thigh, cutting deep. It dropped to one knee, but still snarled, still reached. Rhazha shoved her boot into its chest and kicked it backwards with all the force she had. The orc hit the wall hard and slumped.

'Rhazha!' Adanion shouted. 'Grenade!'

She turned, catching the small, crudely-made device Adanion hurled towards the enemy ranks—a firepowder flask wrapped in cloth and wire. The thing was barely more than a tinker's toy—unstable, wild, and prone to premature detonation. But Adanion was nothing if not resourceful. She caught it with both hands, spun towards the corridor, and saw the cluster of orcs closing fast.

With no time to hesitate, she pulled the pin and tossed the grenade towards the chokepoint in the corridor.

BOOM.

Flames roared, smoke billowed, and debris rained down as the ceiling collapsed, blocking the orcs' path. The explosion rocked the floor beneath them. A shockwave punched through the corridor, throwing Rhazha backwards into the wall. Heat licked her skin, and the flash left spots dancing in her vision. Stone chunks fell from the archway, dust mushrooming outward as beams groaned and gave way. The screams of surprised orcs were swallowed by falling rubble and fire.

Dust filled the air, the acrid scent of burning wood and powder choking their lungs.

'Go!' Rhazha gasped, grabbing Kril's arm and dragging him towards the exit.

He'd taken a hit—his shoulder was soaked in blood, and his footing was off—but he didn't resist. He let her pull him through the fractured doorway, ducking low beneath hanging beams and smoke-streaked rubble. Every breath felt like breathing fire, and behind them, the ruins groaned, threatening to collapse entirely.

They burst through the ruined doorway into the cold night air, lungs gasping for fresh breath. The forest swallowed them like a living thing—dark and infinite. Trees loomed overhead, their branches clawing at the starless sky. A chill wind rustled through the undergrowth, carrying with it the damp scent of earth and pine, a sharp contrast to the suffocating dust and smoke they'd just escaped.

Kril leaned against a tree, clutching a bleeding shoulder, sweat and grime streaking his face. His breath came in battered gasps, each one a struggle as adrenaline slowly drained from his body. The wound was deep, the blood seeping through the fabric of his shirt, but his jaw was set firm. He didn't complain. Didn't even wince.

Adanion slid down beside him, still watching the treeline for any sign of pursuit. His face was streaked with soot and sweat, the faintest twitch of a smile playing at the corner of his lips despite exhaustion. His eyes, sharp and alert, scanned the shadows as if daring any predator to step forward.

'Are you okay?' Adanion asked, his voice rough.

Kril grunted. 'Could be worse.' His hand instinctively

went to the wound again, fingers brushing against the sticky blood. 'But it burns like fire.'

Rhazha looked down at the Emberfang blade, its red glow now faint but steady in her hands. The pulse seemed softer here, as though it knew they were momentarily safe, though the weight of its legacy still pressed heavily on her chest.

'Better now,' she said quietly, though the tightness in her throat betrayed the toll the escape had taken.

Kril handed her a flask, the worn leather soft in his calloused hand. The flask felt heavy with the promise of relief. Rhazha uncorked it and took a slow, deliberate sip. The warm burn of the liquid eased some of the rawness in her lungs and throat.

'Still think this job was easy?' Kril muttered, his voice dry but edged with grim humour.

She gave a tired smile, the tension easing just a fraction. 'You two aren't half bad.'

'Just wait 'til we get paid,' Adanion said, wiping soot from his brow. The smile there was genuine now—brief, but real.

They sat there for a long moment, the distant roar of orcs fading with the night.

The forest seemed to close in around them, alive with sounds that were both familiar and foreign. The rustle of leaves whispered secrets, and somewhere far off, an owl called out—a lonely, mournful cry. The cool night air seemed to draw out the ache in their muscles, the rawness in their spirits.

But the blade's power weighed heavy, like a shadow settled over Rhazha's heart.

She stared down at the Emberfang blade, its dull red glow pulsing steadily in the gloom, the dark runes alive with a magic older than memory. It was more than just a weapon. It was history, blood, and pain forged into an edge sharper than steel—a legacy that demanded reckoning.

Her fingers tightened around the hilt. The cold metal pressed against her skin, yet the blade seemed to hum with heat, a faint vibration that whispered promises and warnings all at once. Rhazha swallowed hard, feeling the gravity of what they had just taken—not just an artefact, but a responsibility.

'Do you ever wonder,' she began, her voice quiet, almost fragile beneath the weight of the moment, 'if some things are better left buried?'

Adanion met her eyes, the flickering firelight catching the hard planes of his face. His usual cocky grin was gone, replaced by something quieter, more thoughtful.

'Sometimes,' he said slowly. 'But you never know until you face them.'

There was a truth there that struck deep. History had a way of clawing back into the present—whether you invited it or not.

Kril cracked his knuckles, the bruises and cuts raw and aching, a slow rhythm to the movement as if steadying himself for what was next.

'We just keep moving,' he said gruffly, his voice steady despite the pain. 'One step at a time.'

The forest whispered around them, alive with secrets and dangers. The night felt endless and watchful, and the weight of the Emberfang blade was like a silent heartbeat in the darkness—a reminder that this was only the beginning.

Rhazha inhaled deeply, letting the cold air fill her lungs. The path ahead was uncertain, tangled with shadows and old ghosts, but she knew one thing: They could never turn back. Not now.

The blade pulsed once more, faint but relentless. It was

alive. Waiting.
   And their journey was far from over.

CHAPTER ELEVEN

A Sword That Whispers and a Campfire That Talks

T HE NIGHT AIR PRESSED IN close, filled with the crackle of embers and the gentle hiss of logs shifting in the fire. Stars peeked through gaps in the canopy, cold pinpricks against a velvet sky. All was still but for the glow of the campfire and the faint murmur of something older lurking in the shadows.

Crickets sang in the underbrush, their rhythms uneven like an anxious heartbeat. The flames offered little warmth; the cold lingered in the soil, twisting through shadows and curling up around boots and sleeping rolls. The trees loomed large above, branches black against the stars. It was the sort of night that made quiet feel like pressure, a living thing settling on their shoulders. A low mist, smelling of damp earth and rot, began to creep through the roots and brambles, obscuring the ground around them in a veil of silver-grey.

The air was thick with the dust of the collapsing tunnels, and the scent of burnt magic hung heavy. They had the Emberfang, a strange and beautiful artefact pulsing with a faint, malevolent light. Rhazha held it with a surprising tenderness, almost as if she were cradling a lost child rather than a cursed object. Her fingers traced the subtle curve of its hilt, not with the intent of a warrior, but with the solemn care of a mourner touching a grave marker. The sword was a physical representation of everything she had lost and everything she had yet to face.

Adanion shifted on the rough log, the weight of the world settling into his bones like the chill in the air. He watched Rhazha carefully—not just the sword glowing faintly in her lap, but her. The way her shoulders tensed and relaxed with the rhythm of the firelight, the subtle tightening around her eyes, the unspoken words caught on the edge of her breath. Nights like this carried ghosts—not those that hid in the dark, but the ones stitched into your own heart, the regrets and failures that followed you like a second skin.

He wondered what it was like to hold a sword that spoke—not just metaphorically, but truly whispered to its bearer. Did it haunt her? Comfort her? Or did it demand more than she could give? He knew that kind of burden well. Not from any sword, but from choices that left scars on the soul. He knew the feeling of being hunted by the person you used to be. The Emberfang wasn't just a physical trophy; it was a soul-tether, a chain linking her to a past she seemed desperate to outrun.

Kril was quiet for once, the usual rough energy of the burly warrior subdued beneath layers of exhaustion. He sat a few feet away, tending the fire with slow, deliberate motions. He'd seen too many nights like this, too many moments of fragile calm before the next storm. His gaze lingered on Rhazha, then on the sword, his brow furrowed in a deep scowl. Even Kril's usual gruffness seemed subdued in the presence of this burden—something heavier than mere exhaustion. There was a weight here that even his strong arms couldn't lift. For all his bluster, he was a creature of simple truths: a good axe, a full stomach, and the loyalty of those who fought beside him. The magic that hummed from the Emberfang, the complex past it represented, was a realm he could not understand, and that made him uneasy.

The fire snapped, sending a shower of sparks upward. Rhazha's fingers twitched over the wrapped sword, tracing the outline beneath the cloth. The faint glow of runes seeped through, a soft pulse like a heartbeat he could almost feel against his skin. She was no longer just the silent, deadly warrior they had hired. She was something more, a puzzle with a thousand bloody pieces.

'That sword,' Adanion said softly, his voice cutting through the crackle of the fire, 'it's more than just metal and magic, isn't it?'

She didn't answer at once. Her eyes remained locked on the weapon, her lips pressed in a thin line. The silence stretched, a taut rope between them, until she finally spoke, her voice a low murmur. 'It's a legacy. And a warning.'

Adanion's gaze lingered on her face—the lines of strain, the flicker of defiance. 'A warning to whom?'

'To anyone who thinks power comes without price.'

For a moment, the forest around them seemed to lean closer, as if eager to catch every word. The wind shifted, carrying the scent of pine and earth—fresh, alive, but tinged with something old.

'You've carried this alone for too long,' Adanion said, voice low but steady. 'You don't have to anymore.'

At last, her eyes left the sword and found his. In their depths, he saw a vulnerability she rarely allowed. 'It's not just the sword,' she said quietly. 'It's everything tied to it. The expectations. The failures. The ghosts.'

'We all have ghosts,' Kril murmured from his corner. 'Some louder than others.'

Adanion smiled faintly, a sad, knowing look on his face. 'Louder ghosts tend to make the best company.'

Kril laughed—a rough, short bark that broke some of the tension. 'I'll drink to that, once we're out of the woods.'

Rhazha's lips twitched with the semblance of a smile, but her eyes stayed wary. 'We're not just running from ghosts anymore. We're being hunted by shadows—things that don't want to be found.'

Adanion shifted again, drawing his cloak tighter. 'I've always found shadows easier to track once they're bleeding.'

There was a pause as the fire flickered, the three of them caught in a fragile stillness. The woods remained still, as if waiting for the next move. Inside, the quiet felt like a fragile thread stretched tight between them—ready to snap, or hold fast.

'What if...' Rhazha asked suddenly, her voice barely above the fire's crackle. 'What if it calls out to the worst in me?'

Adanion's answer came slow, careful. 'Then you show it you're stronger.'

She looked at him then—really looked—and for a moment, the mask slipped. Vulnerability flickered there, quickly masked by steel and resolve.

'Maybe I don't want to be stronger,' she whispered. 'Maybe I just want to be free.'

'Freedom's a strange thing,' Adanion said. 'Sometimes it's the hardest chain to break.'

Kril grunted in agreement. 'But it's worth the fight.'

Rhazha's gaze returned to the Emberfang. 'It's not just a weapon. It's a promise—and a curse.'

Adanion nodded. 'Promises are meant to be kept. Curses... well, they're only as strong as we let them be.'

The night deepened around them, but the fire's warmth felt like a small rebellion against the cold that threatened to swallow everything whole. Rhazha sank further into the log, the sword's subtle luminescence lingering across her lap. The forest's shadows seemed to grow longer, a deep, silent darkness beyond the reach of their firelight.

Adanion watched her carefully, resting his chin on a fist. 'Still talking to you?'

'It doesn't stop,' she murmured. 'But I'm not afraid of it anymore.'

'Is that a good thing?' he asked, a hint of concern in his voice.

She didn't answer at once. She considered the question, her brow furrowed in concentration. The sword's pulse seemed to speed up, a low thrumming against her palms. She felt a whisper of a new kind of power—not the destructive rage she'd felt in the vault, but a colder, more precise feeling. The runes seemed to glow with a hungry intelligence.

'I think it's like hunger,' Adanion said finally, answering his own question. 'You feel it. But you don't have to feed it.'

Rhazha smiled faintly. 'What would you know about that?'

'I buried one once,' he said quietly, voice dropping, green eyes distant. The flicker of the firelight made his face seem older, the lines of past sorrows etched deeper. 'A cursed thing. Wasn't just a trinket. It burned a whole village before I got it under control. People died. I couldn't save them.'

She turned to face him now. The levity was gone, replaced by a profound silence that settled between them. '...And you don't regret it?'

He nodded once. 'Every day. And never at all.'

She blinked at that. It was a paradox that she understood, a knot of conflicting truths that spoke to the heart of what it meant to carry such a burden.

'It's hard to regret what you had to do,' Adanion said, voice low. 'But it doesn't mean you get to stop paying for it.' He ran a hand through his silver hair, a weary gesture. 'Every so often, even now, I check twice before touching a cursed thing, double-check my traps, my spells... my lies. Old ghosts have a way of catching up, whether you invite them or not.'

Her eyes softened for a fraction of a second—enough to betray a flicker of vulnerability beneath the sharp edges she wore like armour. The firelight cast shadows that danced across her face, framing a woman weighed down by legacies not her own, forced to carry burdens she never asked for.

The forest seemed to hold its breath. They sat in silence for a long moment, lulled by the fire's dance. The air was thick with the scent of pine and damp earth, mingling with the faint metallic tang from the Emberfang's runes. The unspoken truths, the shared pain, felt more real than the stone beneath them. For the first time, Rhazha felt a deep, profound sense of camaraderie. They weren't just a team; they were a fellowship of broken things, bound by secrets and the desperate hope of a future they could earn.

Then, a new scent cut through the night—not pine, not earth, but the faint, coppery scent of iron and cold sweat. It was a scent Adanion knew intimately, a smell he had been trained to detect since before he could hold a sword. A subtle scent of blood, old and dry, carried on the breeze from the direction of the crumbling fortress behind them. He stiffened, his hand going to his sword hilt, fingers brushing the familiar leather. Kril's head snapped up, eyes wide and alert, the exhaustion gone in an instant. The half-giant's nose had caught it, too. A low growl rumbled in his chest, a sound like grinding stone.

They didn't speak. They didn't need to. The silence itself had become a warning.

From the forest edge, a flicker of movement—a shadow detaching from the darkness, then another. No sound. No snapped twigs or rustling leaves. Just the subtle shift of something that didn't belong. Rhazha felt the Emberfang pulse a little faster, a tremor of recognition running through its hilt. It was a different kind of magic, a different kind of fear.

Adanion raised his hand, a silent gesture for Kril to stay low, his body tensing for a fight. But the figures didn't move with the lumbering steps of orcs or the heavy gear of mercenaries. They moved with the silent, predatory grace of hunters. They were stalkers, trained in the art of vanishing into the night. Adanion's mind raced, trying to categorise the threat. Not a tracker from the warband—they were too subtle for that. Not bounty hunters—they were too patient.

The first sound was a faint click—something small and deliberate. The trio stiffened, muscles tensing.

The sound came again—another inner branch beneath a heavy step.

They waited. Rhazha's hand tightened on the hilt of the Emberfang, her knuckles turning pale green. The runes flared brighter, a silent protest against the encroaching danger. Kril shifted his weight, his axe, Lorna, resting easy on his shoulder, a silent promise of violence.

The shadows between the trees stirred, as if the forest had exhaled. From the darkness, a figure materialised—silent, cautious, wrapped in muted colours that blended with the night. The ranger's eyes shone faintly beneath his hood, sharp and assessing, trained to catch threats and secrets alike. His movements were fluid, a constant ripple of motion that seemed to defy the very ground he walked on.

A masked figure emerged, the hush of cloth on armour barely audible: a ranger from the Hinterwood patrol, drawn by light and smoke.

'I mean no harm. I was sent by a friend in Mudwater. They thought I might find you here.'

Rhazha exhaled slowly, lowering the blade. The tension bled from her shoulders in a slow, tired wave. 'A friend?'

The ranger stepped forward, face dim, the mask a simple piece of leather with eye slits that gave nothing away. He carried no obvious weapons, only a small pouch at his hip and a bow strapped to his back. His hands were open, a gesture of peace that felt both genuine and carefully rehearsed. 'A man named Tavian. He said you helped him get away from a debt collector with a mean streak and a talent for curses.'

Adanion's face split into a wide grin. 'Tavian! The drunk who lost his pants in a dice game. I told him he should have paid the debt, but he said the collector's curses were just bad poetry.' He laughed softly, the sound a welcome relief in the tense night.

'He still feels that way,' the ranger said, a hint of dry amusement in his voice. 'Mudwater's safe. But the warband is gathering. They'll come for the orc sword at dawn.'

Adanion shrugged. 'Of course they will. We're carrying a legendary, soul-sucking weapon. What else would they do?'

'I can help. I know a path east to the Border Watch. They'll protect you—if you reach them by daybreak.'

Rhazha looked at the blade, then at her friends. The offer was a lifeline, a chance to get to a place of safety. But it was also a choice. She could run again, or she could face what was coming. The Emberfang pulsed faintly against her palm, a question in its rhythmic glow.

'We leave at first light,' she said, her voice a low command. There was no hesitation now. The choice had been made

The ranger's voice held the weight of urgent truth, breaking the fragile calm that had settled over the camp. There was no room for hesitation now; the chase was far from over. The sword, the warband, the clans—all pieces in a deadly game none of them could yet see clearly. But one thing was certain: survival would demand every shred of their cunning and will.

The fire was burning low now, no longer a beacon, just a warm reminder of the life they still carried. The birds had started again—quiet chirps, hesitant, as though they weren't sure if the danger was truly gone.

Kril was the first to doze, arms crossed over his chest, his back resting against the trunk of a moss-draped cedar. His snore was steady and low, like distant thunder. Rhazha sat opposite the fire, the Emberfang lying beside her once again. This time, she hadn't bothered wrapping it completely—just enough to dim the glow of the runes. They pulsed faintly through the cloth like a heartbeat with no body.

Adanion's gaze lingered on her for a moment longer, noting the way her fingers traced absent patterns over the blade's wrapped form. The silence carried the weight of unspoken truths—regrets, fears, and hopes drifting with the smoke towards the stars.

Rhazha finally looked down at the Emberfang. 'Our leader wielded this before... we lost him. When he died, it was sealed away. My clan said it was too dangerous to wield again. That it drew out the worst parts of the bearer.'

'And you went and stole it anyway.'

'I didn't steal it. I recovered it.'

Adanion raised an eyebrow.

She rolled her eyes. 'Alright, I stole it. But it was my responsibility to stop it falling into the wrong hands. I was ambushed by the Black Fang near the Grey Passes. They broke the blade apart and scattered the pieces.'

Adanion chuckled. 'Well, that seemed to work out well,' he said sarcastically. 'But, there it is.'

'Where what is?'

'The real you. Sharp edges and all.'

Her gaze held his for a second longer than necessary. Then she exhaled slowly. 'You really planning to follow me back to my clan?'

'Thinking about it.'

'They're not exactly welcoming.'

'I'm not exactly polite.'

That earned a laugh. A real one, short but warm. She reached for her waterskin, took a sip, and passed it over. He drank.

'I left in disgrace,' she said quietly. 'Abandoned my post. My family. Everything. And now I'm supposed to walk back into their stronghold with this sword and pretend I'm some kind of saviour?'

'No,' Adanion said. 'You walk in and show them who you've become. That's not pretending. That's the point.'

Another pause. Another spark rose into the dark.

'Why do you care so much?' she asked, genuinely. 'You've got no stake in this.'

He smiled, just a little. 'Maybe I like lost causes. Or maybe I'm just curious to see what happens when someone really pisses you off.'

Kril groaned from his half-sleep. 'He likes fiery women.'

Adanion glanced over. 'I thought you were asleep.'

'Trying. Failing.'

'Want a lullaby?' Adanion offered, already picking up a stick like a pretend lute.

'Touch me with that and I break your fingers.'

Rhazha shook her head. 'This is what I'm bringing back. Chaos and sarcasm.'

'Better than silence and shame,' Adanion said.

They let the moment linger, the soft comfort of companionship weaving through the night. Even Kril's rumbling snores felt less intrusive—more like a reminder that, despite the danger, they were still alive.

A stillness settled over them then—not empty, but earned. The flames dwindled, no longer a guiding light, only a quiet pulse of warmth they still possessed. The sky above shifted. Night began to soften at the edges, bruising into purple. Soon, dawn would press through the branches.

Rhazha stood first. She re-wrapped the Emberfang tightly, slung it over her back, and adjusted her gear. Her movements were smooth, purposeful.

'Let's move,' she said.

Kril groaned again but stood.

Adanion stretched, bones cracking. 'You sure about this? One last chance to turn around and live anonymously in a nice coastal village where no one tries to kill us.'

She looked back at him. 'I'm not sure of anything. But I'm done running.'

That was all it took. Adanion nodded and fell into step beside her. Kril trailed behind, muttering about the lack of breakfast.

They slipped into the morning mist, three figures threading purposefully towards Flintspire and the unknown beyond. Behind them, the embers of their campfire whispered to the wind. And deep in the cloth wrapping, the Emberfang pulsed once—quiet, but not forgotten.

CHAPTER TWELVE

The Bounty Problem

The road into Flintspire wound through a corridor of skeletal trees, their branches clawing at the morning sky. Fog clung low to the ground, thick enough to hide a dozen ambushes and thin enough to make you wonder which direction the trouble might come from. Adanion's boots squelched through the muck as he glanced back at the others. They looked like they'd been served to a wyvern and sent back with complaints. Kril's armour was scorched in three places, and Adanion's cloak dangled in tatters. Rhazha dragged one leg with a stubborn limp, carrying her pain like a trophy.

Flintspire loomed ahead, a squat fortress of a town hunched against the grey sky. It greeted them with a chill that felt less like morning air and more like an old grudge. The first light barely touched the uneven cobbles beneath their feet as they crossed the muddy threshold. Guards at the gate gave them the look usually reserved for troublemakers and plague victims. One reached for his halberd until Rhazha shot him a look that made him reconsider his life choices.

They passed under the stone arch and into a maze of alleyways slick with moisture and lined with shuttered windows. A few stray chickens darted past. Somewhere, a smith's hammer rang out like a war drum. Children played a half-hearted game of stones under the watchful eye of a grandmother who looked like she could kill a man with a soup ladle.

'This place smells like regret and boiled cabbage,' Adanion muttered, his half-cloak flapping unevenly behind him like a wounded banner.

'Better than the stink coming off you,' Rhazha muttered back.

Adanion gave her a look that was half-amused, half-offended—and entirely unbothered. He was getting used to her jabs, even enjoyed them, though he'd never admit it.

They kept their heads down and moved quickly through the weary-eyed crowds. It didn't take long to reach the forge district, though getting there without a fight or a mugging felt like a small miracle. Their contact waited near the forge district, where the air smelled of soot, sweat, and hot iron. Morgrin Blackbriar was a dwarf with a beard that probably had its own retirement plan. He stood with arms crossed and an expression that suggested he'd already had three disappointments today and wasn't in the mood for a fourth.

Morgrin's squat frame was hunched slightly, as if the weight of his years pressed down harder than any armour could. His dark eyes flicked over the trio with a mixture of grudging respect and weary calculation. The edges of his lips twitched like he wanted to curse something—maybe the dawn, maybe fate, maybe the elf standing before him with one sleeve hanging loose and a half-smile that said trouble was never far behind.

He wore a leather apron scarred from years of working the forge, though these days his hands were just as likely to be wrapped around a tankard as a hammer. Around his neck hung a crude chain with a small iron gear—a token of craftsmanship, or a reminder of a past life that refused to let go.

'Yer late,' Morgrin grunted without looking up. His voice was rough, like gravel dragged through mud, but there was no real surprise in the tone.

Adanion swallowed a yawn and glanced at Rhazha, who offered a smirk despite the limp.

'Blame the orcs,' Adanion said. 'And the magically cursed talking sword. And that blasted firebomb.'

Morgrin snorted, a dry, humourless sound. 'Talkin' swords are never good news. But I'd expect nothin' less from you two.'

Morgrin eyed the bundle under her arm. 'That the Emberfang?'

'It's whispering obscenities right now, if you want proof.'

He held up a calloused hand. 'I'll take yer word for it.'

Morgrin handed over a thick pouch of coin. It jingled like music to Adanion's ears.

'Payment, as agreed. Plus a little bonus,' the dwarf said, then added darkly, 'and a bit of news that's less pleasant.'

He reached into his coat and pulled out a folded parchment, tossing it to the elf, who caught it one-handed.

Adanion opened it—and immediately started laughing.

It was a wanted poster.

A bad one.

Crude sketches, obviously done by someone who'd never seen an elf up close and assumed they all looked vaguely like insulted cats. Adanion's depiction was all sharp eyebrows and sneering cheekbones. Rhazha's image was worryingly flattering, her braid windswept and eyes smouldering. Kril looked like someone had drawn a rock and given it rage.

'They got your scowl perfect,' Adanion said, nudging

Kril.

'Good,' Kril said. 'They'll see me coming.'

Rhazha arched an eyebrow. 'They made me look like I model for battlefield calendars.'

'Do you not?' Adanion quipped.

She rolled her eyes.

Morgrin scratched his beard. 'Iron Tusks put the bounty out last night. Wanted: dead, preferably. Fifty gold apiece, more if brought in alive and still twitching.'

'I love being popular,' Adanion muttered, folding the poster. 'But I take issue with this artist. They gave me no chin.'

'Maybe they just saw you early in the morning,' Rhazha said.

Morgrin handed her another parchment. 'You'll need to lay low. Change names, if you can help it. Don't go marching into towns with this thing humming doom songs,' he nodded to the Emberfang.

'I'm not good with aliases,' Kril said, eyeing the paper.

'You once told a customs officer your name was Punchy McFight-Face,' Adanion said.

'And he believed me.'

'That's not the win you think it is.'

Morgrin gave them a curt nod. 'Camp outside the walls tonight. Town'll be crawling with bounty rats soon. If I hear anything, I'll send word. And for the love of the Forge, don't start another war in my region.'

'Define "start",' Rhazha said.

The dwarf didn't dignify that with an answer. He turned and stomped off into the morning fog, muttering something about 'pointy-eared arsonists.'

A MODERATE CHANCE OF SCREAMING

They didn't leave Flintspire immediately.

Morgrin had pointed them towards a tucked-away tavern called The Dented Helm, a place so small it barely qualified as a room with chairs. Its sign was missing half the lettering, and the other half had been repainted by someone with more mead than talent. But the fire was hot, the benches sturdy, and the stew thick enough to double as spackle.

Inside, the low murmur of voices kept to themselves. Most of the clientele looked like regulars—men and women who lived by the forge and drank by the fire, each with a face that seemed carved from stone. No one spared them more than a glance.

They took a corner table near the hearth, shadows gathering close like old friends. Kril's massive form barely fit on the bench, and he muttered about dwarven furniture being made for dwarven arses. Rhazha sipped from a chipped tankard with both hands wrapped around it, soaking in the heat. Adanion stirred his bowl of stew and tried not to think about what might be floating in it.

For the first time in days, there was no shouting, no swords, no curses muttered by sentient weapons. Just the quiet hiss of the hearth and the creak of old wood settling into night.

'I still smell like burning orc,' Adanion muttered, sniffing his sleeve.

'That's because you do,' Rhazha said, not looking up.

He smiled faintly. 'Good. I'd hate to lose the scent of victory.'

Kril took a long gulp from his mug. 'Smells more like scorched Aevrinai and desperation.'

'Adds character.'

'You don't need more character,' Rhazha said, setting her tankard down. 'You need soap.'

He looked at her, mock-wounded. 'That's hurtful.'

'And accurate.'

Despite themselves, a thin line of amusement tugged at all three mouths.

Outside, Flintspire carried on—rough, weathered, and unforgiving. But here, for a heartbeat, the world eased. The bench was hard, the drink cheap, and the stew suspiciously chewy, but it was warm. And it was theirs.

Kril leaned back against the wall, the low crackle of the fire brushing against his heavy breaths. Rhazha rolled her shoulders with a sigh, as though trying to release the weight of everything she wasn't saying. Even Adanion's endless restlessness stilled, his gaze flicking towards the fire instead of the door.

No plans. No blades drawn. Just a pause.

Just long enough to remember what quiet felt like.

They made camp just past the eastern ridge, among a sparse stretch of wind-whipped trees. Flintspire was still visible in the distance, its rooftops little teeth on the horizon. The sun sank behind the hills, bleeding gold into a sky bruised with dusk.

Kril sharpened his axe again, each scrape of the whetstone rhythmic and soothing in the way only weapon maintenance can be when your day job involves stabbing people for a living.

Adanion leaned back on his elbows, staring up at the first stars. 'You know, it's not every day we get immortalised on official parchment.'

'Immortalised?' Kril asked.

'Well, I mean, badly drawn and semi-literate, sure. But it's a start.'

Rhazha sat cross-legged with the Emberfang laid across her lap, still wrapped in its cloth. She hadn't said much since they left Flintspire. Her face was unreadable in the firelight—caught between exhaustion and something deeper, something quieter.

'I hate being hunted,' she said finally.

Adanion glanced at her. 'You get used to it.'

'You would.'

He smiled but didn't argue.

She traced one finger along the edge of the cloth, not touching the sword directly. 'It wants blood. That's how it remembers. That's how it stays awake.'

Kril paused his sharpening. 'You're not planning to feed it, are you?'

'No. But someone will. Someone always does.'

A heavy silence followed. The kind that pressed against your ribs.

Night deepened around them, the fire crackling softly as embers drifted upward into a sky thick with stars. Kril's breath came steady in sleep, sprawled out on the makeshift cot beneath a patchy blanket. The wounds from their recent battle throbbed beneath his armour, but fatigue had claimed him fully.

Adanion rose quietly, the chill in the air pushing him towards the small stream a short walk from the camp. The water promised some relief, a chance to wash away the grime and blood smeared across skin and cloth.

As he splashed the cold water over his face and neck, the muscles in his back tensed and relaxed with each breath. The night was quiet except for the gentle murmur of the stream and distant calls of night birds. He closed his eyes, letting the cold steal some of the ache from his bones.

Nearby, Rhazha had set up a small basin and was washing

the grime from her arms, the cloth wrapped tight around the Emberfang resting beside her. She moved with a practised grace, each motion precise, careful—a stark contrast to the ferocity she'd shown hours before.

Thinking she was alone, Adanion stepped towards the shelter they'd built. But as he rounded the corner, the faint sound of a cloth dropping and a sharp intake of breath made him freeze. He hadn't expected her to be there, much less without her usual armour.

For a heartbeat, their eyes met—hers steady, unflinching, a flicker of something unreadable passing through her dark gaze. The firelight painted shadows across her skin, revealing the lines of muscle and scars that told their own stories.

Adanion swallowed, heart thumping loud in the still night. He turned away abruptly, the awkwardness settling between them like thick smoke. But the moment lingered— electric, charged, unspoken.

Later, by the dying firelight, they sat closer than before, each nursing a mug of bitter stew and strong drink. Their hands hovered near, brushing briefly before pulling away, fingers twitching with words they didn't say. The night seemed to lean in, listening to the silence between them.

No promises were made. No confessions whispered. Just the slow, inevitable pull of something waiting beneath the surface.

The fire crackled, embers floating up like sparks from a hidden flame—a flame neither dared fully kindle yet.

Eventually, Adanion said, 'So what's next? We vanish into the woods? Change names? Let Kril try aliases again?'

'Damn right,' Kril said. 'This time I'm going with 'Murderton Beefslam.'

Rhazha gave a short laugh, her first in hours. 'You're an idiot.'

'And proud.'

'We need a plan,' Adanion said. 'Lying low only buys time. That bounty won't vanish unless someone makes it.'

'You volunteering?' Kril asked.

Adanion shrugged. 'We've got a sword that screams history and bad decisions, and a clan of orcs who think we owe them blood. Might as well face it.'

Rhazha set down her mug, voice low. 'I used to think I'd die in a pit fight. Crowd screaming, blood in my teeth. That was the dream once.'

'Bit grim,' Adanion said.

'Bit honest.'

He nodded, eyes on the fire. 'I thought I'd fade out on a forgotten battlefield. Arrow through the ribs. Name on a stone no one visits.'

Kril grunted. 'I wanted a forge. Quiet, steel, maybe a goat or two.'

That almost drew a laugh, but it passed. Silence settled, not heavy but earned, the kind that only came after fire and flight.

The fire burned low, no longer a beacon, only warmth. Around it they sat—criminals, outcasts, wanted names—but also a team.

Rhazha's gaze lingered on the flames. 'I'm taking it home,' she said at last. 'To my people. Even if they hate me. This blade can't stay a weapon. I want it to be a key.'

Adanion leaned towards her, steady. 'Then we'll go with you.'

Kril nodded once. 'Not done yet anyway.'

She looked between them, surprised, but found no jest in their faces—only resolve.

Adanion stirred. 'Strange company we make—Aevrinai, Orzhaan-blood, Hryndahl. Hardly the kind of company bards sing about.'

'Depends who sings it,' Rhazha said.

'Kril,' Adanion smirked. 'Drunk. Off that Hryndahl swill.'

'Fermented heritage,' Kril muttered, and this time Rhazha chuckled, just enough to ease the stillness.

The fire popped softly. The birds began again, cautious in the dark.

Rhazha lifted her chin. 'Then we make it worth singing.'

They took shifts through the night, keeping watch while the others tried to sleep. The forest around them was alive with unfamiliar sounds, shadows shifting just beyond the firelight's reach. Each snap of a twig made them flinch, every rustle of leaves a possible threat.

'I don't like this,' Kril muttered as he passed the flask to Rhazha during his watch.

'Neither do I,' she said, taking a small sip. 'But we don't have a choice.'

'Maybe we should've stayed with the Iron Tusks,' Kril joked bitterly, but there was no real humour behind it. 'Their wrath runs deep—more than just the usual grudges. There's talk the clan's been stirred up, restless after... well, after what happened.'

Rhazha's eyes flicked to the darkness beyond the fire. 'They want more than heads. They want a message sent.'

The hours crawled by, and as dawn began to break, Adanion crouched near the fire, running a hand through his hair.

'We'll need allies,' he said quietly.

'Sure,' Kril replied. 'Because everyone in this world loves a bunch of wanted fugitives.'

Adanion smiled wryly. 'Sometimes desperation makes people listen.'

Rhazha looked towards the horizon, the first rays of sun casting gold over the trees. 'We don't get a second chance. If I don't fix what I broke... well, none of this matters.'

Her voice cracked, just barely, but it was there.

Kril clapped a heavy hand on her shoulder. 'We'll get through this. Together.'

And for the first time that night, Rhazha allowed herself a small, hopeful smile.

That day, they slipped through Flintspire's back alleys, eyes down, ears open. The bounty posters were everywhere—nailed to walls, pinned to bulletin boards, shouted about in the marketplace.

'Looks like we're not the only ones wanting to collect,' Adanion muttered, dodging a suspicious glance from a grizzled merchant.

They passed a pair of mercenaries whispering in a corner, their hands twitching towards weapons.

'We're not safe anywhere,' Rhazha said quietly.

Kril's fingers tightened on his axe. 'Then we make our own safety.'

The bounty was more than just a price on their heads. It was a message—a reminder of the danger that chased them, and the consequences of crossing the Iron Tusks.

And now, more than ever, they needed to be sharper, faster, and smarter.

Because the hunt was just beginning.

CHAPTER THIRTEEN

ASHES OF THE HEIR

T*HE CITY'S WALLS HAD VANISHED* behind them, swallowed by the forest's endless green, replaced by the hush of ancient trees and the scent of damp earth. Mist clung to the roots and brambles like reluctant ghosts, curling around gnarled trunks and slipping silently between their boots. Every footfall whispered, and every shadow seemed to watch.

Adanion's eyes swept the forest with habitual caution, nostrils flaring against the faintly acrid smell of moss and rot. He wiped sweat from his brow, but it did little to ease the tension coiling in his chest. 'We're being hunted,' he said flatly, his voice low enough for the trees to carry it but not the enemy. 'Not just Iron Tusks. Others are here too. Bounty hunters, mercs... maybe worse.'

Kril's jaw tightened, knuckles whitening around the haft of his axe. 'Iron Tusks don't care for subtlety. But if others are tracking us, this bounty's bigger than we thought.' His voice carried a gravelly weight, like stone pressed against steel. His eyes flicked constantly from shadow to shadow, catching every twitch of leaf or shadowy movement. Even the wind seemed to hush when he focused.

Rhazha walked ahead, Emberfang strapped across her

back, its crimson cloth barely moving beneath the pale light of a sun filtered through dense branches. Her fingers curled lightly around the hilt as though it might fly off if she let go entirely. 'Gharok the Burnt's followers won't stop until they reclaim that blade,' she said, voice low, tight with memory. 'They're ruthless.'

Adanion tilted his head. 'Gharok the... Burnt? Someone you know?'

Her eyes darkened, pain flickering like candlelight behind her gaze. 'He was more than an enemy once. The Emberfang... it changes those who wield it. I've seen what it does. I've seen what it does to him.'

The forest pressed closer, branches clawing at cloaks and hair, moss weighing heavily on bent limbs. The undergrowth muffled their steps, but also swallowed sound, creating a sense of false security. Even the distant burble of a stream seemed tentative, like it didn't dare announce its presence. Adanion noticed the stillness, the way the mist moved—almost intentionally, brushing past them, curling around the bases of trees as though inspecting their passage.

Kril's movements were subtle but constant. Every step he took was measured, deliberate, like a predator half-hidden in plain sight. He sniffed the wind, shifted weight quietly, eyes narrowing at something unseen. Adanion, familiar with the half-giant's instincts, felt the hair on the back of his neck prickle.

The trio slowed only when the forest thinned near a narrow stream, the water gurgling softly over stones slick with moss. Its faint song was a balm against their ragged breaths, a momentary comfort that the world still held pieces untouched by cruelty.

They pressed deeper into the ruins, where ancient stone walls rose from the forest floor like the bones of a long-dead giant. Pillars jutted at odd angles; walls were half-swallowed by ivy, inscriptions eroded beyond recognition. The air felt thicker here, heavy with dampness, dust, and the quiet echo of memory. Kril dropped to a crouch near the edges, eyes sweeping over the broken ground, muscles coiled and ready.

Adanion settled a small fire, just enough to cast flickering shadows across the crumbled walls. The light was insufficient to warm, but enough to illuminate faces and the tense lines of bodies prepared for violence. Rhazha sat apart, Emberfang across her knees, thumb brushing its hilt in a constant, almost unconscious rhythm.

Adanion studied her. 'You've gone quiet—and you're thinking. That alone worries me.'

She exhaled, a weighty, measured sound, like wind over the ruins. Her gaze swept him, then Kril, and rested finally on the fire. 'You think Gharok's just going to welcome me back because I've got a shiny sword?'

Kril's grunt cut through the night. 'Did cross my mind.'

'He won't,' she said. 'That's not the point.'

Adanion's brow furrowed. 'Then what is?'

She paused, letting the wind carry her words. Leaves stirred overhead, shadows shifting across her face.

'He killed my father,' she said, her voice bare, raw. 'Chained me, helpless... forced me to watch as he tore him apart. The air reeked of blood and smoke, thick and choking. I can still see the look in his eyes as the life left him—while that bastard just... smiled.'

Her fingers tightened on Emberfang's hilt, her green knuckles blanching pale, hands trembling despite her grip. A single tear cut a path through the grime on her cheek before she savagely wiped it away with the back of her hand.

'He took my mother and me in chains, like we were possessions, like we belonged to him. Called me his daughter, but I wasn't his child. I was a prize. A toy. A lesson. He raised me like a trophy with teeth, shaping me in the shadow of his cruelty. Said I would be his little legacy... his *heir*.'

The fire crackled. Adanion's usual half-smile was gone, replaced by a grim line. His gaze dropped to his hands, staring as though he'd never seen them before. Across the flames, Kril's axe haft groaned under his grip. He did not look at either of them, but fixed his eyes on the darkness beyond, his breath slow and heavy, each exhale thick with rage held in check.

Rhazha's eyes darkened, distant, unblinking. Her voice fell quieter, though it struck harder than any shout.

'He came for me too, as he did my mother. Meant to shape me, break me, make me his. Every day, every lesson, every threat... all to prove I belonged to him. That I could never be my own.'

Adanion said nothing. The fire crackled, its warmth failing to reach his spine.

'But I didn't let him finish,' she continued, jaw tight, voice quiet but unyielding. 'I ran before he could claim the rest of me. Before he could make me... what he wanted. I survived. I waited. And I came back. Not as his toy, not as his trophy. Not as his "heir".'

Kril's gravelled voice came from across the fire. 'And now?'

Rhazha's thumb traced a faint edge on Emberfang. 'Now I go back. Not to reclaim a name. Not to rule. But to prove I'm not what he made. And to remind him that I will never be what he made me. What he tried to make me.'

Her hand moved from the sword, slipped beneath the edge of her leather armour, and retrieved a small, iron coin from a thin, sewn pouch flat against her ribs. It was pitted with age, the symbol of a half sun and half skull worn smooth by years of handling. She held it tight in her palm, letting the cold metal ground her. This coin had belonged to her father, the last Chieftain before Gharok the Burnt took his life. It was a secret she had carried through every chain and every threat, and seeing it now, the worn symbol was proof: her vengeance was not just personal; it was blood right.

Adanion swallowed, knowing the battle ahead wasn't just for the sword, or the tribe, or survival—it was personal. And it was already burning.

The forest grew thicker as they pressed on, the trees bending over the path like gnarled fingers. Moss dripped from the branches in long, wet strands, clinging to their cloaks and hair. Every sound was magnified in the hush: a snapping twig, the rustle of leaves, the soft drip of water from stone to stone. Even the wind seemed hesitant, as though it feared stirring something hidden.

Kril's eyes were relentless, sweeping left and right, scanning the shadows for movement. He moved like a shadow himself, low and deliberate, every step measured. Adanion followed, one hand brushing the hilt of his sword while the other lingered near the silver ring in his pouch—a talisman he hadn't trusted anyone else with.

Rhazha led the way, Emberfang strapped across her back. Her posture was taut but controlled, a predator in human form. Even the mist seemed to part around her, brushing at her ankles like hesitant smoke. Adanion could feel the pull of her presence, the way the air around her shimmered with restrained energy. He knew that quiet before a storm, and it made his gut tighten.

The ruined outcrop rose ahead, half-swallowed by ivy and

forest rot. Moss-covered stone steps twisted upward at odd angles, leading to what had once been a hall or watchtower. Pillars jutted like broken teeth from the earth, some toppled, some leaning precariously, etched with symbols worn smooth by centuries. The ruins seemed alive in their stillness, holding the echoes of the past like a memory too stubborn to fade.

Adanion gestured to Kril and Rhazha, lowering his voice. 'Keep your eyes sharp. We don't know what's waiting.'

Kril nodded, tightening his grip on Lorna. 'They're close. I can smell it.' His voice carried a tension Adanion had only heard before in the quiet moments before a hunt.

They moved carefully, one foot in front of the other, weaving through the stone columns and shattered walls. Every creak of broken wood, every faint shuffle of leaves, seemed to mark the presence of something watching. Adanion's fingers itched for the sword he carried at his side, for the first strike that would give him a sense of control.

The first warning came as a whisper—a soft scuff of boots on stone, barely audible over the rustling leaves. Adanion froze, eyes scanning. Two figures darted between the ruins' shadows, moving with silent precision, blades drawn. His breath hitched, muscles coiling.

'Trap,' Rhazha murmured, her voice barely audible, but it cut sharper than any sword.

It sprang.

Shadows lunged from both sides—silent, fast, deadly. Adanion barely had time to duck the first strike, steel grazing his shoulder. Kril was already moving, a coiled whirlwind of strength, meeting two attackers head-on, snarling as he sent one crashing into stone.

Rhazha didn't hesitate. She drew Emberfang, her grip

already firm, but something in her posture changed. Her movements tightened, growing more deliberate, as if she were feeling the weight and power of the blade for the first time. Her thumb brushed the glowing runes, and she gave the sword a sharp twist in her hand, the sudden flash of power a promise and a threat. She pulled the heart-shaped crystal from her belt pouch, the cool stone a stark contrast to the heat of the chase. With a sharp twist, she pressed it into the hilt of the Emberfang. It snapped into place with a subtle click, and a jolt of raw power slammed into her, an almost painful surge of energy. The dark crystal followed, sliding into its own waiting socket with a whisper of magic. The runes on the blade flared brighter, and the air around them filled with the scent of ozone and fire.

The sword erupted into flame as she swung, arcing through the nearest attacker's gut. Smoke rose, the scent of iron and fire mingling in the cool evening air. The man crumpled to the ground, half ash, half ruin, and she didn't pause.

The attackers pressed on, a second wave, more feral than the first. Their movements were uneven, desperate, but coordinated enough to force the trio apart. One bore a chain leash; at the other end, a hulking tusked beast with iron-spiked muzzle snarled, straining at its bonds. Its dark eyes tracked Rhazha, calculating and furious.

Adanion's sword met a heavyset mercenary in chainmail over leathers. Sparks flew with each clash. He ducked under a mace swing, drove his blade into the man's side, and felt the satisfying give of flesh. Another came at him before he could catch his breath.

Kril's axe sang through the chaos. Lorna crashed against bodies, bone and sinew, giving way to raw power. One attacker screamed as Kril caught her axe with his boot, ripped it free, then drove his own through the ribs. Two more came from either side—he took them down with a single, hammering sweep. The stone was slick with blood, but Kril didn't pause, didn't falter.

Through the maelstrom, Rhazha moved like wind through fire. Every strike was final, precise, fuelled by more than skill—by the history of her pain, the weight of every lesson forced upon her by Gharok. Emberfang burned with a heat that was older than flame, war-tempered, hungry for vengeance.

Adanion darted through the fray, limbs moving with the deadly grace of a predator. He caught a blade mid-swing, twisted, drove his sword through the attacker's side. The fight was relentless; even the smallest pause could mean death.

And yet, amidst it all, Rhazha's eyes never wavered. She wasn't merely defending herself or her companions—she was declaring, through every swing, every parry, that she belonged to no one.

The scarred leader shouted from the rear, a cruel rasp that carried over the clash of metal. 'Rhazha. You cannot hide. Emberfang belongs to Gharok!'

Her breath hitched, but her resolve did not. She spun, a streak of red and gold in the dim light, cutting down one attacker, then another. Each strike was a lesson remembered, a wrong avenged, a chain shattered in blood.

Adanion saw it then: this wasn't just a fight for survival. It was her reclaiming herself, carving out a space in the world where Gharok's shadow could not reach. Every attacker who fell wasn't just meat on the ground—it was a mark of her freedom.

The beast lunged, chain snapping as it charged. Adanion leapt to intercept, shouting her name. She waited, Emberfang poised, eyes aflame. At the last second, she pivoted inward, driving the sword beneath its jaw. The tusked creature choked, crashed sideways, and lay still. Silence fell.

The remaining attackers fled, leaving blood-soaked stone and curling mist in their wake. Adanion approached, cautious. 'You all right?'

She let the sword rest in her hands, pulse glowing faintly. 'He taught me to fight,' she said. 'Gharok. Said it would make me useful.' She wiped Emberfang clean on her sleeve.

'Instead, it made me free.'

Mist curled around broken stone and scattered bodies, hugging the earth like a reluctant witness. Rhazha knelt, letting Emberfang rest against her knees, breathing ragged but steady. Her hands shook faintly—not from exhaustion, but from the hollow silence that followed fire and steel.

Adanion crouched beside her, glancing across the ruins. 'That was... impressive,' he said, but his voice lacked its usual levity. 'You're ready for him, then.'

She met his eyes, something flickering—defiance, fear, memory. 'Ready? No. But I won't let him finish me.' Her fingers brushed Emberfang's hilt. 'Not now. Not ever.'

Kril, standing near the edge of the arch, surveyed the perimeter, axe resting loosely on his shoulder. 'We need to move soon. They'll send more, or worse.'

Rhazha nodded. The forest seemed alive, shadows moving with a mind of their own. She shivered, not from cold. 'Every step towards him... it's a reminder of what he took. But it's also... proof. I'm still standing.'

Adanion exhaled, running a hand through his hair. 'And we're still standing with you. That counts for something.'

Silence fell again, thick with unspoken truths. The mist thinned slowly, revealing glimpses of the jagged hills where Gharok's stronghold awaited. Somewhere beyond, he was planning, scheming, unaware that she would return—not broken, not bowed, but sharp and ready.

CHAPTER FOURTEEN

THE FALL OF THE BURNT

T HE PLAN WAS SIMPLE: RHAZHA would return the Emberfang to her tribe, Kril and Adanion would wait nearby, and maybe no one would die.

Naturally, everything went to hell within ten minutes.

From the cover of the ridge, Adanion's keen eyes tracked Rhazha's lone figure as she made her way down the rocky slope towards the orc warcamp. The sword was carefully wrapped in crimson cloth in her arms, its weight a heavy reminder of the stakes they were gambling with. She walked with the heavy grace of a warrior returning from exile, head held high but shoulders burdened.

The morning mist clung to the trees below, weaving between twisted branches like silent watchers, as if the forest itself was holding its breath. The wind carried distant shouts and the clang of metal on metal, punctuating the tense stillness around them. Somewhere down there, death waited.

Kril, beside Adanion, squinted against the rising sun. 'Why aren't they stabbing her?'

Adanion's brow furrowed. 'Because they're letting her talk. Which means... wait.'

The orc chieftain, Gharok the Burnt, lumbered forward from the shadows of a massive war tent, his scarred face twisted into something almost like a smile as he reached for the wrapped blade.

Adanion's voice dropped. 'Well, that's not good.'

Kril smirked, cracking his knuckles. 'What tipped you off?

Seconds later, Rhazha found herself surrounded, a flash of steel and raw anger. She fought like a cornered wolf, slashing and dodging, but she was hopelessly outnumbered.

Adanion cursed under his breath. 'We've got to go in.'

"Bout damn time,' Kril growled, shoulders rolling as he readied his axe.

The orcs closed in like a pack of wolves, snarling and snapping, their eyes wild with bloodlust. Rhazha's breath came hard and sharp as she twisted on the balls of her feet, Emberfang's crimson cloth fluttering like a banner of defiance. Every swing she made was a calculated arc of death, carving paths through the enemy with ruthless precision.

Around her, the clash of steel rang out in savage rhythm—blades meeting bone and metal, the grunt of exertion, and the wet thud of flesh succumbing to steel. Each moment was a blur of motion; the sickening crunch of broken ribs, the hiss of blood spraying through the air, the gritty taste of dirt and sweat mingling on Rhazha's tongue. Her muscles screamed in protest, but her grip on Emberfang never wavered. She was a storm contained in a single body, relentless and burning.

A snarling orc lunged, his jagged blade aiming to rip through her side. Rhazha twisted low, her boots scraping against loose stones, rolling beneath the savage arc. The scrape of rough earth bit into her palm, sharp and unforgiving, but she pressed the advantage—driving the tip of Emberfang deep under the ribs of her attacker. The orc collapsed in a spray of blackish-red, his guttural howl dying in a choked cough. Rhazha barely spared him a glance, already pivoting to meet the next threat.

Above, on the ridge, Adanion's pulse thundered in his ears, the tension coiling tighter with every heartbeat. He drew his sword, the weight familiar and grounding, and sprinted down the rocky slope, each footfall pounding a war drum against the earth. Beside him, Kril moved like a living tempest, the glint of his axe catching the first rays of sun like a predator's fang.

They crashed into the fray as a cyclone of steel and fury, their war cries tearing through the air and shattering the orcs' momentum. Adanion instantly grabbed a discarded orc buckler from the churned dirt, using it to parry a clumsy javelin thrust, before ducking a savage overhead swing meant to cleave his skull, rolling sideways with a grace born of years on the battlefield. His blade flashed, a lethal streak of silver, slashing fiercely across the exposed throat of his foe. The orc staggered, clutching at the wound as blood bubbled between his fingers.

Kril's axe sang a terrible song—a biting, deadly note as it bit into the skull of a snarling attacker. Bones shattered beneath the force of the blow, and Kril laughed—a savage, primal sound that echoed like thunder. He pivoted on blood-slicked stone to meet a spear thrust aimed for Rhazha's back.

'Not today!' Kril roared, launching himself between the spear and her just in time. The weapon slammed into his shoulder, searing agony exploding through his body like wildfire, but he stood firm. Gritting his teeth, he wrenched the spear free and slammed the butt of his axe into the attacker's gut with a crushing thud.

Rhazha's eyes burned with molten iron as she pivoted

towards the chieftain's second-in-command—a hulking brute whose scarred face twisted into a cruel sneer. Their blades clashed with a thunderous clang, sparks flying in the humid morning air as steel met steel. The brute pressed hard, each strike heavier, more desperate.

She ducked under a wild swing and countered with a vicious slash that tore open a deep gash along his arm. The orc roared, staggering back, blood pouring from the wound, staining the dust beneath him.

From the chaos, Adanion caught sight of Gharok weaving through the melee, his voice rising above the din with sharp commands that sent fresh waves of orcs crashing into the fight. His eyes gleamed with wicked amusement—a predator savouring the hunt.

Nearby, a dagger-wielding orc lunged at Adanion, aiming for his throat. He twisted aside just in time, the blade slicing the air inches from his skin. Grabbing the attacker's wrist, he spun him off balance and drove the flat of his blade across the orc's face. Blood sprayed in a cruel arc, splattering the rocks beneath their feet.

Kril's breath was ragged; blood trickled freely from his shoulder wound. Yet still, his axe fell with deadly force, felling orc after orc. 'For the tribe!' he bellowed, a primal roar that stirred a fierce fire in Rhazha's chest.

The battlefield was a whirlwind of fury and chaos—flashes of steel, cries of pain, the acrid scent of sweat and iron thick in the air. Dust choked their lungs, and the sun beat mercilessly down, turning the ridge into a furnace of violence.

Step by step, they carved their way through the enemy ranks, bodies slick with sweat and streaked with grime and blood. Rhazha's muscles screamed, but her hold on Emberfang was ironclad. Every strike was a promise—a vow to carve a path to the chieftain himself.

Suddenly, Gharok stepped forward, scars on his face twisting into a grimace of rage. His great axe swung in a wide arc, forcing Rhazha to leap back. The blade crashed into the boulder where she'd stood moments before.

Adanion surged forward, shield raised, blocking a brutal overhead chop aimed at Rhazha. The force sent him staggering back, but he held firm, teeth clenched.

For a heartbeat, the battle seemed to pause—then the earth trembled beneath their feet, a deep, rolling quake that sent dust and loose stone skittering across the ridge.

Through the haze lumbered a colossal, armour-plated warbull, its tusks curving like hooked spears.

Rhazha's breath caught, her grip tightening on Emberfang. 'Mokgar,' she spat, the word carrying the weight of deep familiarity.

The beast bellowed and charged. His war hammer smashed into the earth, hurling shards of rock into the air. Kril surged forward with a thunderous roar of his own.

'Mine.'

'Good idea,' quipped Adanion.

Without hesitation, the half-giant launched himself forward, each step shaking the ground like the fall of a mountain. 'Been too long since I fought something that didn't break easy.'

Mokgar charged, a living battering ram. His iron-stone war hammer swung in a brutal arc, smashing into the earth where Kril had stood seconds before, sending a geyser of shattered rock and dust skyward.

Kril crashed away from the blow, slamming into the remnants of a broken cart. Wood splintered beneath him, but he pushed up on bloodied hands, lips curling into a savage grin.

'Come on, tusk… You have to do better than that.'

The orc beast bellowed, a sound that shook the bones of everyone on the ridge, and surged forward again. Kril rolled to the side, narrowly evading a second thunderous hammer blow that smashed into the earth with shattering force.

But the third strike caught him. The hammer clipped his ribs, a searing crack echoing as the ground exploded nearby. Kril grunted, eyes watering, breath ragged—but his fury only deepened.

He answered with a brutal hook, fist smashing into Mokgar's massive jaw. The orc's head snapped back, but the beast merely laughed—a guttural, terrifying sound that was half beast, half war cry.

Mokgar slammed his spiked forehead into Kril's chest, the impact driving the half-giant backwards like a battering ram, slamming him against a gnarled tree. Wood cracked and bark shredded as the two titans clashed.

Mokgar's hammer crashed down with a roar, splintering the earth where Kril had stood a moment before. The half-giant twisted, iron sinews straining, the shockwave rattling his bones. He countered with a savage punch to the beast's snarling snout, teeth gnashing.

Kril caught Mokgar's wrist just as the war hammer swung down again, wrenching it—only to be thrown like a ragdoll against a stone pillar.

Dazed but unbroken, Kril spat blood, his voice a low snarl. 'Adanion, you seeing this? I'm getting a workout.'

'Wouldn't miss it for the world,' Adanion called, weaving through orcs to stand near the fray. 'He hits like a landslide!'

Kril grinned fiercely, fingers clenched tight around his axe handle. 'When this toothy bastard is down, I'm coming for that rotten chieftain.'

The war-bull roared, fury blazing in his eyes as he swung

wildly, the hammer smashing the earth again and again. Kril ducked and dodged, each movement a desperate dance between death and defiance.

Seizing a moment, Kril drove the spike of his axe low—burrowing into Mokgar's thick thigh. The beast howled, staggering, claws scrabbling for purchase on the rocky soil.

Kril charged, tackling the monster from behind, muscles burning with raw, primal strength. They crashed to the ground with the force of an avalanche, Mokgar thrashing wildly, but Kril locked his arms tight around the beast's throat.

'Fall, damn you!' Kril growled, grinding his teeth against the wild resistance.

Mokgar slammed him into the earth again and again, but Kril held fast. Finally, with a brutal roar, Kril twisted free, dropped low—and brought his axe crashing down with savage finality.

Bone cracked, and the war-bull's guttural roar died to a wet gurgle as he collapsed, twitching in the dust.

Kril rose, battered and bloodied, breath coming hard. He wiped a smear of crimson from his lip and gave a weary, bloody grin.

'Told you. Mine.'

Adanion surged forward, glancing at Rhazha. 'Go, Rhazha!' he yelled, his voice sharp. 'He's not the one you came for!'

Her heart thundered as she slipped past them, every step carrying her closer to the black shadow at the ridge's heart.

Gharok.

The battlefield seemed to exhale around them—the tide of the orcs swayed with the loss of their monstrous champion.

Yet Gharok the Burnt stood firm, a twisted grin carving his scarred face.

His great axe gleamed with cruel intent, eyes blazing with dark promises.

'You think you can face me?' he snarled, stepping forward through the carnage. 'I took your father's Emberfang, crushed him like a beetle. You, little Rhazha, are nothing but a broken shadow. And you...' his gaze snapped to the half-giant, 'will learn what it means to be crushed underfoot.'

Rhazha's grip tightened on Emberfang, its crimson cloth snapping like a banner of rebellion. Pain and fury burned in her eyes—a fire kindled long ago by loss and torment.

'You made me run, Gharok,' she said, voice cold as steel. 'You thought you'd break me. But I'm still standing. And today, I claim my vengeance.'

The air thrummed with the clash of steel as the trio surged forward—Kril's axe swinging in powerful arcs, Adanion's sword flashing with deadly precision, and Rhazha's Emberfang weaving a deadly dance of fire and death.

Gharok met them with brutal strength and skill, every strike a testament to his dark mastery. He fought like a storm—relentless, merciless—each blow meant to break and dominate.

But the trio moved as one, their attacks striking true and hard, their resolve unyielding.

Adanion ducked a wild, savage swing, grinning as he jabbed, 'Ever consider you're a bit too angry for your own good?'

Kril roared, 'I'm angrier!'

Rhazha's eyes burned with fierce resolve, each strike a poem of retribution, a reclaiming of her shattered legacy.

But Gharok was no ordinary foe—his blows hammered like thunder, his presence a dark storm that sought to drown her will.

Suddenly, a deep roar split the chaos—a thunder from the ridge above. Through the smoke and shattered stone, a grim-faced band surged forward.

Morgrin Blackbriar, axe swinging with brutal precision, led a cadre of battle-hardened warriors—grim men and women wielding swords, axes, and bows, faces set in unyielding determination.

Their war cries ripped through the din, a rallying cry that struck hope like lightning into the hearts of the weary defenders.

The tide shifted. Orcs wavered, faltered, then fled before the onslaught. The allies' arrival fractured the horde's relentless surge, buying precious moments.

Kril, bloodied but unbowed, staggered back beside Rhazha. She knelt beside him, her breath ragged but her gaze fierce.

'We live to fight another day,' she said, voice steady despite the ache in her limbs.

Adanion clapped Kril's shoulder, a grin breaking through the grime. 'Next time, you're letting me land the first blow.'

Kril chuckled, wiping sweat and blood from his brow. 'You? I'd rather face Mokgar again.'

Yet even as their brief respite settled over them, Rhazha's mind churned with the weight of memories. The crushing loss of her father—fierce and proud, felled by this very monster. The shadow of her mother's suffering, broken and beaten beneath Gharok's tyranny.

She was not just fighting for survival. She was fighting for reclamation—for breaking the cycle of pain and fear that had haunted her since she was a child.

Slowly, her gaze hardened. The Emberfang pulsed in her hand, its crimson edge a beacon of hope and vengeance.

Gharok stirred, rising like a dark colossus, eyes burning with rage and disbelief.

Rhazha steadied herself. This fight was far from over.

For a heartbeat, the world seemed to pause—just long enough for the dust to swirl between them, for the clang of steel and the screams of the wounded to fade into the background hum of war.

Then came the roar.

Not just from Gharok—but from the hundreds of orcs swarming down the far ridge, their war cries splitting the sky like thunder. The horizon darkened with their approach. Waves of them, snarling, bristling, blades raised and eyes gleaming with the lust of violence. A wall of hate and muscle, bearing down to crush the last breath from the trio who dared defy the Burnt.

'So much for subtle,' Adanion muttered, wiping blood from his brow.

'Told you,' Kril grunted beside him, brandishing his axe like a mountain made war-ready.

'Could've just let me throw her at the problem.'

Rhazha didn't hear them. Not really.

She stared ahead at the monster who had haunted her nightmares, a monster no child should have had to kneel before.

Gharok stepped through the carnage like a god of ruin. His armour was scorched black and jagged like cooled magma, each plate spiked and carved with symbols of dominance. The great axe in his hands was nearly as tall as Adanion, its cruel blade jagged from use and stained from unspoken horrors.

His eyes were pits of fire, one burning red with hate, the other milk-white and blind, narrowed with hateful amusement as he looked at Rhazha—not as an enemy, not even as a warrior. As a possession that had dared to disobey.

'You look like her,' he called out, voice gravel-thick and oily with intent. 'When she still fought me. Before she broke.'

Rhazha's grip on Emberfang whitened.

'But *you* felt better,' he said with a grin.

The memory hit her like a second blade: her mother, defiant even as her spirit was choked out over months of captivity. Gharok had crushed her. Slowly. Purposefully. Until the last ember flickered out—and he had turned to Rhazha.

But she hadn't broken.

She had run.

And now she was done running.

Gharok beckoned with a tilt of his head, like calling a dog. 'Come then, girl. Come show me how well you remember your training.'

The words snapped like a whip in her mind. Rhazha moved.

She launched herself forward, Emberfang slicing through the air like a scar of fire. Their weapons collided with a shuddering crack, the force sending tremors through her shoulders. Sparks exploded as their blades ground together—then again, and again—metal shrieking like tortured ghosts.

Gharok drove into her with monstrous strength. Every strike was a storm front, every step a siege. He laughed as he fought, a deep, hideous thing that made her skin crawl. He wasn't just trying to kill her—he was enjoying it.

'I shaped you,' he snarled, forcing her back with a flurry of brutal swings. 'You were meant to obey me. Serve me.

Kneel when I commanded. To become what I carved into you.'

'I'm not yours,' she spat, ducking a blow that cracked stone. Emberfang whipped out, scoring a red-hot line across his thigh. 'And I never was.'

'You will be.'

He lunged.

They crashed together in a storm of blades, teeth bared and muscles screaming. Emberfang hissed as it met the corrupted iron of Gharok's axe. For every step Rhazha took forward, he knocked her two back. He was a juggernaut, unrelenting, dragging her towards the same pit he'd dragged her mother.

Adanion carved through the press of bodies, eyes locked on Rhazha—but the horde sealed around him like a vice. Ten orcs surged at once, blades flashing, snarls rising. He turned, cloak whipping, sword a blur of desperate precision.

To his left, not twenty strides away, Kril waded through blood and wreckage, his axe cleaving through torsos like a force of nature.

'She'd better kill that bastard!' the half-giant bellowed, slamming an orc into the dirt with a crunch. 'Or I'm eating his face myself!'

Adanion ducked a wild swing, drove his blade into a throat, and spat blood from his lip. 'Leave me a toe! For luck!'

Their laughter was raw, edged with exhaustion because they were losing ground—but still defiant.

The horde was too large. Too relentless. For every orc they felled, five more surged forward, snarling, screaming, fanatical.

And in the heart of it all, Gharok was only getting stronger, his power seeping into them like a storm gathering behind a single, monstrous will.

The orcs kept coming.

Gharok fought like a war god, and his rage was contagious—feeding their ranks, igniting every blade and boot and scream.

Wave after wave crashed against the crumbling line, blades ringing, arrows hissing, war drums pounding like thunder beneath the skin. The sky churned with smoke and ash, and the ridge trembled under the weight of iron and death.

Kril roared, swinging wide in a brutal arc that took down two, three—then staggered as a spear gouged his thigh. He snarled, yanked it free, and hurled it through a charging warrior's chest.

Adanion spun in close behind him, parrying high, slicing low. 'We're thinning them!'

'You're dreaming,' Kril spat, blood running down his leg. 'We're drowning.'

Ahead, beyond the crush of bodies and broken stone, Rhazha fought alone—locked in a storm of steel and memory. Gharok was relentless, hammering at her guard with strikes that could shatter bone. Emberfang flared in her hands, its crimson edge blazing as it met the jagged bite of his axe again and again.

He was toying with her now. Pacing her. Punishing her. Driving her back.

'You'll break,' he hissed, circling, grinning, voice slick with triumph. 'Like she did. Like they all do.'

Rhazha's teeth bared. Her shoulder screamed with every parry, knees buckling under the weight of his blows—but her eyes never left his.

'I'm not her,' she growled.

'No,' Gharok said, slamming his axe down like a guillotine. 'You're weaker.'

The impact crushed her to one knee. Her breath tore free in a ragged gasp.

Across the battlefield, Kril turned—just in time to see her fall.

NO!'

He surged forward—only to be slammed back by a wall of orcs that spilt from the flank. Dozens now. Maybe hundreds. A tide of blades and boots. They were being swallowed.

'Dani!' he barked. 'We can't hold this line!'

Adanion blocked a slash to the ribs, staggered, then stabbed clean through an orc's eye. He saw Rhazha too—struggling to rise, the Emberfang flickering like a dying star.

And still, she fought.

Around them, the battlefield erupted in a savage tempest of steel and blood, Orcish war cries colliding with the clash of blades and the roar of shattered shields. Yet within that chaos, the world seemed to contract—time slowed, sound dulled—until nothing remained but Rhazha and Gharok, locked in a primal, violent ballet.

He was the dark storm incarnate: brutal, relentless, a monstrous force forged in cruelty and conquest. She was the flickering flame that refused to be snuffed, the last ember of a legacy burned nearly to ash.

Their swords met again and again—Emberfang's crimson edge singing a deadly song against Gharok's brutal, savage strikes. Sparks flew like fireflies caught in a gale, each collision echoing like thunder through the war-torn air. The ground beneath them cracked and trembled, bearing witness to their fury.

Behind her, Kril and Adanion stood like unyielding sentinels, axes and blades a whirling tempest of destruction. Orcs pressed forward in desperate waves, but none could breach their iron wall. Each swing, each brutal strike from the towering half-giant and the agile Elven swordsman carved space for Rhazha, a bulwark forged from blood and iron.

Her arms burned, muscles screaming, but every movement carried the weight of a thousand memories—her father's proud stance, her mother's whispered prayers, her own years of torment and survival. Each strike was no longer merely survival; it was defiance incarnate, a roaring declaration that she was no longer prey to fate.

Then came the scream.

Not one of fear—but of fury, of pain transmuted into power, of every stolen year returned in defiance. It ripped from Rhazha's chest like the roar of a dragon waking after a long, cursed sleep. The battlefield seemed to pause in reverence, as though the very earth recognised something ancient in her cry.

Gharok raised his axe for a final, killing blow—an arc meant to end her, to crush her into the dirt as he had crushed so many before. But she moved with the fluid certainty of someone who no longer doubted her right to fight. Emberfang spun in her grip, catching the firelight with every motion, until it wasn't a blade—it was a comet.

And then she struck.

With the force of her bloodline behind her—the echo of her father's fall, and the fury of her mother's last breath—Rhazha drove Emberfang into Gharok's chest. Deep. Unforgiving. Final.

The blade flared like molten fire.

It burned through flesh and shattered bone, searing straight into the heart of the monster who had tried to unmake her. The crimson edge of Emberfang ignited like a flare in the darkness, the crystals embedded in the hilt of the blade pulsing violently. For a heartbeat, it was not just a weapon—but a judgement. A reckoning.

Gharok reeled, choking on disbelief.

His mouth opened to roar, but only a strangled gasp escaped. His eyes—those pits of hate and conquest—found hers, wide with a shock he'd never known in battle. The cruel grin he wore like a crown fractured. Cracks split across the mask of brutality that had once made him a god to his followers. In that moment, he wasn't the Burnt. He wasn't the warlord, or the executioner, or the nightmare.

He was just a man now.

A dying man, stripped of power and pretence, staring at the child he thought he'd broken—no longer a god, no longer a warlord, just a shadow fading into dust.

The storm inside him collapsed. Power fled his limbs. His axe slipped from his fingers, thudding into the churned, blood-soaked earth. He staggered, limbs twitching, mouth trembling with something that might have been a curse—or a plea.

But Rhazha said nothing.

She tore Emberfang free with a twist that sent fire bursting from the wound, and Gharok fell to his knees like a crumbling statue, eyes still locked on hers. The towering monster who had haunted her for years—who had buried her childhood and twisted her fate—sank to the ground before her, hollowed of rage, emptied of power.

Rhazha stood over Gharok's broken form, chest heaving, limbs shaking from the tempest of battle and the surge of newfound strength. The acrid scent of blood and fire filled the air, but beneath it all, a quiet reckoning settled deep in her bones. She looked down at the ruin of the monster who had tried to claim her soul—and something in her, something heavy and old, finally exhaled.

Her shoulders trembled from the weight of what she'd done. Of what she'd finally undone.

This was no longer vengeance.

This was reclamation.

She was not the child who had knelt in chains. Not the girl who had run into the dark. She was the heir of fire and fury—reborn in blood, reborn in blaze, and standing tall beneath a sky that no longer bore his shadow.

Emberfang still glowed faintly in her grasp, its searing fury banked to a slow, pulsing ember.

Around them, the orc horde's roar faltered—then cracked—then shattered completely, splintering like glass beneath the fall of their dark lord. The tide of war broke and scattered, their savage will crumbling to dust.

What had charged like thunder now fled like leaves before a gale. Fear surged through their ranks. The heart of their darkness had been pierced, and with it, the spell of domination undone.

A heavy silence settled like ash over the field.

Rhazha didn't move.

Emberfang still glowed faintly in her grasp, its searing fury banked to a slow, pulsing ember. Gharok lay still beneath her, the weight of him already sinking into the churned soil. Around them, the battlefield had quieted—not with peace, but with the raw, hollow stillness that follows devastation.

A low whistle cut through the silence.

Kril stepped forward, soaked in blood and sweat, one hand dragging his axe, the other pressed to a gash on his ribs. His broad chest rose and fell like bellows, and for a long beat, he simply stared at Gharok's corpse.

'Well. I'll be damned.'

He looked at Rhazha—not the blade, not the body, but her. Eyes sharp despite the bruises, blood trickling down one temple, but upright. Whole. Changed.

'You did it,' he said, voice rough with something that might have been reverence. Or pride.

Adanion approached more slowly. He hadn't sheathed his blade yet. His eyes swept the battlefield first—measuring, confirming. Then he turned to Rhazha, his expression unreadable for a moment.

'Are you hurt?' he asked.

She blinked, as if coming back to herself. Her grip on Emberfang slackened slightly.

'No,' she said, voice hoarse. 'Not anymore.'

Adanion nodded, but he didn't lower his blade just yet. His gaze flicked once more to Gharok's corpse. 'He really is dead?'

'He's not getting back up,' Kril muttered.

A beat passed.

Then Adanion exhaled and let the tension roll from his shoulders. He turned, surveying the broken field. Orc bodies littered the ground—some still twitching, most not. The few remaining fighters were scattering now, without cohesion or orders; the horde dissolved into chaos.

'We should move,' he said. 'Before the next fools try to rally.'

Kril grunted. 'I'm not carrying you both if we have to run, so if anyone's bleeding out, speak now.'

Rhazha gave a small sound—half breath, half laugh—as she finally lowered Emberfang. The blade's glow faded further, retreating into its forged heart. Her legs shook once beneath her, and for a moment, it looked as if she might crumple where she stood.

Adanion caught her arm.

'Easy,' he murmured.

She nodded, breath catching. 'I'm all right.'

'You don't have to be. Not just yet.'

She didn't reply. But she didn't pull away, either. She let his hand stay there. Let the heat of it remind her she hadn't imagined any of this.

Kril bent down with a grunt and retrieved something from the ground. Gharok's war axe. Its weight seemed different now. Duller. Like a crown torn from a corpse. He looked at it for a moment, then tossed it aside into the mud without ceremony.

A breeze rolled over them, carrying the stench of fire and blood. In the distance, Morgrin's voice barked orders, rallying the last of the allied fighters. The battle hadn't just turned—it had ended.

And they were still standing.

Rhazha finally moved. Just one step forward. Her gaze dropped. Gharok's eyes stared upward—lifeless, unseeing. Whatever darkness had driven him was gone now. All that remained was a husk of cruelty, collapsed into the dirt like any other man.

She exhaled.

It was not triumph. Not release. It was… recognition. A quiet, soul-deep knowing that some part of her story had finished here.

She turned back to the others, her jaw set, her face unreadable.

'We need to see who's left,' she said. Her voice was rough, low, but it didn't shake. 'Help where we can.'

Kril gave a curt nod. Adanion hesitated a second longer, his gaze lingering on her with something unreadable—worry, maybe. Or awe.

Then he followed.

Together, they walked into the smouldering remains of the battlefield, weapons lowered, shoulders squared. Not as fugitives. Not as prey.

But as survivors.

The acrid smoke hung low, curling like a living thing around shattered trees and broken bodies alike. The metallic tang of blood mixed with the bitter scent of scorched earth, seeping into the heavy, still air. Silence settled over the field—broken only by the ragged, uneven breaths of survivors, the distant barked orders of Morgrin's voice cutting through the haze as he marshalled his dwarf warriors and allied scouts.

Rhazha's gaze swept across the battered ranks. Men and women of many tribes—some limping, clutching wounds that still bled dark and slow, others frozen in stunned disbelief, faces pale beneath grime and sweat. No cheers rose here, only the weight of loss pressing down like a suffocating shroud. And beneath it all, a quiet pulse of something harder: the hard-won truth of survival.

Morgrin stood atop a fallen stump, his broad frame solid against the smoke-streaked sky. His voice, low and commanding, cut through the quiet like a blade. 'Form ranks! Shield the wounded! Scouts, circle the perimeter. Watch for stragglers. This fight isn't over 'til every enemy is accounted for.'

His warriors moved with unwavering discipline, hands steady even as exhaustion shadowed their faces. Some knelt to tend bleeding wounds with grim efficiency, others sharpened blades or reinforced barricades from broken branches and shattered shields. The mix of battle-hardened men and women—dwarves, humans, and others—stood as a solid anchor amidst the swirling chaos.

A MODERATE CHANCE OF SCREAMING

Nearby, Rhazha's eyes caught a cluster of orcs—scarred and ragged, bloodied but alive. They stared at her with wary, tired eyes, some nursing wounds that might never fully heal, others gripping crude weapons with fingers still trembling. These were the fractured remnants of Gharok's horde—lost their lord, but not their fierce pride.

One stepped forward—a woman marked by scars and fierce eyes that still held fire beneath the weariness.

'You killed the Burnt,' she said flatly, voice rough from shouting and loss. 'We're alive 'cause of you.'

Rhazha met her gaze, feeling the weight behind the words. 'The Emberfang goes back with me.'

The woman nodded once, a brief flicker of respect—and something unspoken—passing between them.

Kril grunted, hauling Gharok's war axe from the mud. 'Good. We'll need every hand if there's more coming.'

Adanion crouched, his sharp eyes sweeping the tree line, muscles tense beneath bloodied leather. 'More could still come. Scouts or stragglers. We need to move fast—rest, regroup, heal.'

Morgrin's voice cut in, gruff and unyielding. 'We'll burn the dead before nightfall. Can't have rot or beasts sniffing around.' He nodded at Gharok's body. 'And his corpse... gets no honour. Just fire and forgettin'.'

Rhazha didn't argue. She knelt beside Gharok's broken form. Fingers trembling, she searched the folds of his tattered cloak and found it—a small, silver pendant shaped like a dagger blade, etched with a fading half sun, half skull, blackened with age and crusted with blood. Her mother's. The last piece of a life stolen, now returned.

Holding it tightly, she rose. Around her, the warriors began to gather dry branches and brush. The woman who spoke earlier struck a flint, sparks catching quickly. Flames licked hungrily at the pyre, smoke curling towards the heavy sky.

Rhazha watched the fire consume the twisted heap that had once been a tyrant. No words, no ceremony. Just the harsh reckoning of war.

She turned to Kril and Adanion, feeling the weight of everything she had lost—and everything she was ready to claim.

Her story was hers now.

And it was only just beginning.

The low fire rustled, its glow casting long shadows across the hollow. The Emberfang rested beside Rhazha, still faintly warm, its light dimming at last.

A scout approached, breath misting in the cold. One of Morgrin's, judging by the battered scale coat and the Blackbriar crest burned into his shoulder plate. He dipped his head in respect.

'Message from the old goat,' the scout muttered. 'He's fortifying the pass with what's left of the shield wall. Says he'll hold it long enough for you three to vanish over the ridge.'

Rhazha nodded, gaze unreadable. 'Tell him we'll be gone by nightfall.'

The scout offered a quick salute and vanished back into the haze.

Kril broke the silence, rolling his shoulder with a grunt. 'Let the old bastard play wall guard. We're the ones who knocked the tower down.'

He looked towards Gharok's pyre in the near distance—flames flickering, smoke rising thick and dark into the dimming sky.

'Still feels wrong,' he muttered, voice lower now. 'Burying a beast in fire. Like dressing a corpse for a coronation.'

Then he shrugged. 'But if that's what keeps the stink down, burn the bastard twice.'

Adanion gave a soft snort, but his gaze was on Rhazha. She hadn't moved since the scout left—sitting quiet, forearms braced on her knees, head bowed slightly as if still listening to something only she could hear.

He watched her, not with the light humour he used to wield like a blade, but with something quieter. Respect, certainly. But layered beneath it—caution. Maybe even fear.

She had changed. Or perhaps, she'd simply removed the mask she'd worn since the night they met.

Rhazha exhaled and rose.

'We leave soon,' she said, brushing ash from her palms. 'The Emberfang doesn't belong in this mud. It belongs where it started.'

Adanion stepped closer, but didn't touch her. 'What then?'

She looked towards the mountains.

'Then I go home,' she said.

Kril grunted. 'Assuming home doesn't try to kill you for returning with their sacred talkin' blade.'

Rhazha gave a ghost of a smile. 'They can try.'

A silence settled—brief, heavy. Then Adanion said, softly, 'And us?'

She didn't answer for a moment. Then:

'You come with me. Just until the gate.'

Kril raised an eyebrow. 'Long enough to carry your body back when they skewer you, got it.'

'Or to make sure I don't skewer them,' she muttered.

That earned a low chuckle.

The three of them began gathering what little they carried—packs, weapons, fresh bandages for the wounds they'd ignored until now.

Behind them, the fire rose higher. Gharok's body would be ash by morning.

And in its place, something new had begun to breathe.

Night crept in slowly, brushing charcoal shadows across the wreckage of war. Fires crackled low among the shattered trees, their glow softening the jagged outlines of what had been—broken weapons, abandoned banners, blood-soaked earth cooling under a darkening sky. Smoke hung heavy, a ghost of the battle that refused to drift away.

Most had gone quiet now. The wounded lay where they could, tended by quiet hands. The dead were being gathered—stacked or buried, depending on what the ground would allow. The air held a strange stillness. Not peace, exactly, but something close. A breath held between what had happened and what came next.

Rhazha sat a little apart, Emberfang across her lap, its light dimmed to a slow ember-glow. She stared not at the blade, but beyond it—towards the trees, towards the mountain, towards something unseen. Her expression was unreadable. Not grief. Not relief. Something older. Worn.

Kril crouched near the fire, using a broken piece of shield to scrape blood from his axe. Adanion stood nearby, watching as stars broke through the soot-dark sky, his gaze fixed on the horizon as though expecting it to shift.

No one spoke for a long while.

Then, as if summoned by some unspoken agreement, they rose—tired, but steady.

Behind them, the last flames of the battlefield flickered low.

And somewhere beyond the trees, a road wound back towards Flintspire.

CHAPTER FIFTEEN

Loot, Loose Ends, and a Sexy Orc

Back in Flintspire, the bustle of the town hummed faintly through the evening air. Horses stamped impatiently in the yards, their restless hooves striking stone and dirt in an eager rhythm. Merchants called out their last wares before sundown, their voices a patchwork of fatigue and determination. Nearby, the clang of a blacksmith hammering a fresh horseshoe rang sharp and metallic, cutting through the murmur of conversation and the occasional bark of a town guard.

The heavy scent of smoke and pine mingled with the sharp tang of freshly turned earth near the town gates. It was there, in the grim shadow of those walls, that Gharok the Burnt had once sat shackled in thick iron chains. The hulking orc's frame had barely fit the cage meant to hold him. His scarred face was a map of grudges and defeat, etched with deep lines from battles past, and the recent loss that had brought him low.

But now he was gone—dead, finally freed from the chains that had bound him. The echoes of his last roar still seemed to linger in the stones beneath their feet, a reminder that even a fallen beast could leave scars that would not fade with the setting sun.

Across the town, deep beneath the ancient fortress walls, the Emberfang rested. The sword lay secured under layers of iron and stone, its crimson-wrapped hilt folded carefully beneath the watchful gaze of Rhazha. Her sharp eyes tracked the flickering torchlight, one hand resting lightly on the sword's sheath, the burden of victory pressing down on her shoulders.

For all the relief it brought, victory had its own burden. In the silence of the vault, it clung to her like a second skin—one as heavy and unyielding as the iron bars that had once caged the orc.

The soft sound of footsteps broke the stillness. Morgrin entered, a battered flagon in one hand and a rough-hewn wooden cup in the other. His beard was tangled with soot and streaked with grey, but his eyes—bright and mischievous beneath thick brows—held a warmth that softened his rough exterior.

'So,' he said, setting down the flagon with a satisfying clunk, 'you've done the impossible. Again.'

The room was small, barely more than a storeroom repurposed for their war council. Wooden crates marked with merchant sigils sat stacked in corners, and a rough table bore the scars of countless meetings. Kril was already perched on one of the crates, his axe resting across his lap. The exhaustion in his eyes did little to dull the dry chuckle that escaped him.

'Just another Tuesday,' he muttered, the corner of his mouth twitching upward despite the weariness drawn into every line of his face.

Adanion lifted his cup with a wry grin, the pale firelight catching the glint of silver at his fingers. 'To improbable odds and overly dramatic exits,' he toasted.

The mugs clinked together, the sound ringing through the quiet space like a promise—and perhaps a warning.

Rhazha lingered by the door, shoulders squared, her posture rigid, though the weariness in her jaw betrayed the fight etched deep into her bones.

When she finally stepped forward, the weight of their shared battle settled between them—unspoken but understood. Her footsteps were soft against the stone floor, each one measured against the memory of the day's bloodshed. She carried herself with the quiet dignity of one who had stared down death and walked away, but her eyes flickered with uncertainty—like the embers of a fire still smouldering beneath ash.

Morgrin nodded in respect, his smile softer now, more knowing. Kril shifted, his usual rough edge dulling as he glanced towards her with something like relief. Even Adanion's grin faltered for a breath as he met Rhazha's gaze, searching for the unspoken truth beneath their hard-won victory.

The room felt smaller now. The shadows heavier.

Morgrin poured a round of ale, the rich, bitter scent filling the air as he passed the cups around. The sound of liquid splashing into wood felt louder somehow, cutting through the silence like a knife.

'Flintspire won't forget this day anytime soon,' Morgrin said quietly, his voice worn by the gravity of the moment. 'You earned more than coin.'

He paused, eyes shadowed in the firelight. 'Strange, not hearing his roar anymore. Flintspire feels quieter without Gharok.'

Kril grunted, rolling the ale in his cup. 'Quieter's good. I'd had enough of that beast's breath to last me a lifetime.'

Adanion gave a faint smirk, though his eyes didn't quite

match it. 'Aye. Though I'll admit, he made for a hell of an exit.'

Rhazha's lips pressed into a thin line. Her voice was steady, but her hand slipped beneath her armour, briefly touching the iron coin flat against her ribs—a reminder of the true cost of the blade now sealed away. 'Chains, blood, fire... he carried them all to the end. But now he's gone. And Flintspire stands.'

She continued, the steel beneath the fatigue unmistakable. 'We rest tonight. Tomorrow, we ride.'

The small room seemed to shrink even further, walls closing in under the weight of unspoken thoughts. Outside, muffled sounds of Flintspire's evening chorus filtered through thick stone—a distant dog's bark, a wagon's creak, footsteps hurried in fading light. Yet inside, the air was still, heavy with exhaustion and the residue of violence.

Morgrin took a slow sip from his cup, eyes flicking between the three figures gathered here. His face bore the lines of countless battles, but there was a spark there—something stubborn, defiant, even hopeful. 'Not many would've made it through the day's chaos without breaking.' His voice lowered to a rough murmur, 'Least of all a half-giant, an elf with a penchant for trouble, and an orc who's earned every scar she wears.'

Kril pulled up a chair, the old wood groaning beneath his weight. He reached for the remaining half-mug and took a swig, then wiped his mouth with the back of his hand.

Morgrin nodded slowly, his voice low and thoughtful. 'There'll be songs about this. Might not get the names right, but the fire'll be real.'

Kril grunted in agreement, resting his axe on the floor.

'Aye. We've earned this one. Might not last, but for now, I'll take it.'

Adanion leaned back in his chair, eyes on the low flicker of firelight. 'Let the world chase its chaos for a while. We've done enough running.'

Morgrin smiled faintly and raised his empty cup. 'To flame-wielders, fool plans, and friends who don't let you die.'

Each mug was raised in solemn tribute, the last of the ale catching in the candlelight.

The firelight flickered and danced along the walls, casting long shadows across their faces—painting doubt, fear, and defiance in equal measure.

Silence stretched for a few heartbeats as they each sat with the weight of it—the blood they'd spilt, the narrow path they'd walked to get here, and the scars that would follow them long after the bruises faded. The fire popped softly, sending a brief flare of sparks drifting into the smoky air.

Kril leaned back against the wall, arms folded behind his head, legs stretched before him. Lorna was close at hand, as always, but for once it didn't seem like an extension of his body—a simple weapon resting by his side. One he was glad not to be swinging.

'You know,' he rumbled, eyes fixed on the ceiling beams above, 'I think this is the first time in weeks I've felt warm without someone trying to kill me.'

Morgrin chuckled, low and gravelly. He slid a heel of bread across the table towards Kril. 'Might be the first time you've eaten something that wasn't smoked field rat.'

Kril glanced down at the bread, then back at the dwarf. 'You're assuming that's not what this is.'

Adanion snorted, slouching with one leg over the arm of

his chair. He tapped a finger thoughtfully on the rim of his mug. 'We should name the rat, if we're going to eat so much of it. Make it more personal. Maurice, maybe.'

'Maurice the rat,' Rhazha said drily, arms folded as she leaned against a beam. 'Had a good run.'

'He died as he lived,' Adanion added solemnly, 'under-seasoned.'

Morgrin rolled his eyes and reached for the flask again, refilling his cup and then Kril's. 'Keep it up, and I'll start crying. The kind of tears that require more ale.'

They drank. Not deeply. Not with the wild abandon of survivors chasing numbness. But with the measured, grateful silence of those who had seen the worst and still drawn breath. The kind of drink that honoured the fallen—and kept the living from forgetting why they'd fought.

'Feels strange,' Kril murmured after a while, eyes half-lidded. 'No blades. No screams. Just a roof. A fire. Food that doesn't try to kill you from the inside.'

'You make it sound like we're retired,' Rhazha said, though there was a ghost of a smile behind the line of her mouth.

'Never said that,' he replied. 'Just... resting. Like soldiers do between wars.'

Adanion's smile dimmed, becoming something quieter. He glanced across the table at her. 'Feels like the eye of a storm. Everything is calm, but only for now.'

Rhazha said nothing at first, just looked into the flames. Her fingers brushed the edge of her belt, where Emberfang had rested before being sealed away again. Her voice came low. 'Then we make the most of the calm.'

She stepped forward finally, easing into the light. The

others shifted to make room. She didn't sit—not yet—but the circle tightened slightly, as if her presence pulled them closer without a word.

'We made it out,' Morgrin said, raising his mug. 'That counts for something.'

'Counts for a lot,' Adanion agreed, eyes still on Rhazha. 'We made it out together.'

Adanion met her eyes, a flicker of the old spark returning. 'Where to?'

He asked it lightly, but the question hung heavy in the air. Not just a matter of direction. A matter of purpose. Of identity. They had fought, bled, and nearly broken—and now they stood at the edge of a world that would never look quite the same.

Rhazha's eyes didn't waver. Her eyes bore the lines of fatigue, a shadow beneath their fierce gleam, but something steadier had kindled there too. A weight she had accepted. Not shouldered alone, but claimed nonetheless.

Her smile was brief—fierce and knowing, shadowed by the burden of leadership. 'Wherever trouble finds us next. I doubt Flintspire will hold its peace for long.'

Soft, bitter laughter passed between them. They had fought through fire and blood, but none of them believed peace was waiting just around the bend.

Morgrin shook his head with a dry chuckle. 'I'll bring the next round. And maybe a feast, if we live long enough to deserve it.'

Kril met his eye. Though exhaustion dulled him, a flicker of hope slipped through. 'Only if you promise not to get us drunk enough to forget what it cost.'

Adanion raised his cup again, his eyes bright beneath tired lids. 'To blood, to gold, and to the bonds that hold us. May they never break.'

Rhazha caught his gaze, the corner of her mouth lifting despite the weariness. 'Or maybe just bend a little.'

Morgrin raised his mug. 'To bending—but not breaking.'

'Aye,' Kril said, his voice low. 'We've done enough breaking for one lifetime.'

The fire crackled as Adanion leaned back, stretching his legs towards the warmth. 'We should've died a dozen times over. Instead we're here, drinking like we earned it.'

'Didn't we?' Rhazha asked, tilting her head.

'Maybe,' he said. 'But sometimes I wonder how much of us made it out of that fight intact.'

'Enough,' Kril rumbled. 'We're still standing. Still breathing. And we still know who the enemy is.'

Morgrin smirked. 'Anyone trying to take my ale qualifies.'

'Speak for yourself,' Adanion said, nudging him with his cup. 'I'm rarely nervous.'

'Because you're rarely thinking,' Kril muttered.

That earned a chuckle, low and tired, from all of them.

Adanion shook his head, eyes narrowing at the fire. 'Still. Not the worst company to share a fire with. Could've ended up dead in a ditch with a goblin in my boots.'

Morgrin snorted. 'You say that like it hasn't happened before.'

'It has,' Kril said flatly.

Rhazha raised an eyebrow. 'You two need supervision.'

'Not wrong,' Morgrin said, then lifted his mug once more. 'To the mad bastards still breathing.'

Adanion's eyes lingered on the others, a quiet weight behind his smile. 'We started off chasing gold. Ended up with a war. I don't know what we are now.'

'Not quite friends,' Rhazha said.

'Not quite mercs,' Kril added.

Morgrin shrugged. 'Something in between. I'll drink to

that.'

Their mugs knocked—wood on tin, dull and uneven—but the sound rang with something solid. And they sat there, letting the words settle like ash after battle.

The fire hissed softly, its flames reduced to glowing embers that flickered with every whisper of air. The heavy scent of burnt wood mixed with sweat, dust, and ale lingered in the room, hanging like a fog over the gathering. Their bodies bore the marks of the day—scrapes, bruises, dirt—but the exhaustion beneath it was heavier, deeper than mere muscle weariness.

Morgrin's calloused fingers trembled slightly as he gathered the empty mugs from the rough-hewn table, the tapping of wood on tin barely breaking the silence. Each step, each movement, was slow and deliberate, as if the smallest noise might shatter the fragile bubble of calm they had carved out amid the chaos of their lives. The weight of survival was a constant, a burden that pressed against their chests with the weight of stone.

Kril's great frame slumped in the corner, the lines of his face drawn tight with fatigue but softened by the glow of the fire. He stared into the flickering light as if searching for answers there, though none came. The gold they had claimed lay secured, but the threat that shadowed them had not lifted. Flintspire's walls kept them safe only for a moment; beyond them, the hunt would resume.

Adanion sat with his back against the stone wall, fingers drumming idly on the mug beside him. His sharp eyes were distant but alert, catching the movement in the firelight and the faint creak of the wooden beams above. He was the youngest of the group, but his mind ran ahead, turning over possibilities and plans with a restless energy that neither the ale nor the weariness could fully quell.

Rhazha's presence near the hearth was a quiet anchor. She sat with her knees drawn close, hands folded loosely on her lap. Her amber eyes caught the firelight, glinting with a fierce light that didn't quite reach the tired lines around them. Though she was no stranger to hardship, there was something in her stillness that spoke of battles fought inside as well as out.

The night pressed in around them, thick with unspoken fears and tentative hope. Each knew the road ahead was uncertain—no grand promises of safety or victory were made here. They sat not as victors, but as survivors sharing a brief respite in a relentless storm.

The firelight danced across their faces as the night stretched long and uncertain before them—but it was theirs to face together.

Morgrin gathered the empty mugs, his fingers sticky with ale as he stacked them. The room fell into quiet once more, the kind that comes not from peace, but from the weight of survival.

Outside, the evening deepened. Stars kindled one by one in the navy-black sky above Flintspire.

Rhazha rose, her boots scraping gently on the stone floor. 'I'm going to check the horses,' she said, her voice steady but low.

Adanion stood as well, stepping after her. 'I'll come with you.'

The others exchanged knowing glances, but said nothing. They understood the unspoken need—after all the fire and blood, a moment of quiet. Of something that felt like normal.

A MODERATE CHANCE OF SCREAMING

Outside the fortress, the chill of night had settled over Flintspire. The scent of pine sharpened in the cold air, mingling with the faint smoke drifting from dying hearths and campfires. Horses stamped and whinnied in the stables, restless, their breath steaming in the dark.

Rhazha moved with calm precision, her hands steady as she tied the reins of a sleek black mare. The animal's muscles twitched beneath a glossy coat, ready for whatever journey lay ahead.

Adanion leaned against the fence, watching her with an expression somewhere between amusement and admiration.

'So,' he said, voice low and teasing, 'now that you're a tribal hero, you'll be too busy for reckless adventures?'

She smirked, a flicker of mischief in her amber eyes. 'Probably,' she replied. 'Unless someone shows up at my tent with a bottle of Blackroot wine and no trousers.'

Adanion's grin widened, firelight catching the sharp edge of his jaw as he stepped a little closer.

'I can work with that.'

They shared a brief, charged silence, then the moment broke with a familiar grunt and the scrape of boots on gravel.

Kril appeared around the corner, dragging a wooden crate that clinked with the unmistakable weight of gold.

'We leaving or what?' he called, his voice rough but edged with a smile.

Rhazha spun on her heel, claiming Adanion's lips in a fierce, searing kiss—wild and urgent, a spark that promised everything and nothing all at once. When she pulled back just enough to whisper, her breath ghosted over his pointed ear.

'Try not to die,' she murmured, voice low and thick with challenge.

He gave a lazy shrug, voice thick with charm. 'Where's the fun in that?'

As she turned to walk away, Kril chuckled. 'You know she's an orc, right?'

Adanion didn't take his eyes off Rhazha's retreating form—each sway of her hips a silent invitation, every step dripping with effortless confidence. The curve of her bare neck caught the fading light, the faint glint of muscles taut beneath her sun-kissed green skin, and the subtle, dangerous grace in her movement that made it impossible not to watch. His grin came slow, a knowing curl that promised trouble.

'Orzhaan, brother mine. And a damned sexy one at that.'

ACKNOWLEDGEMENTS

This book was written under the benevolent influence of strong tea, questionable drinking, edible eating (mostly), several dubious life choices—which may or may not have involved said edibles—and the infinite patience of a handful of people who absolutely had no reason to stick around but did anyway.

To my parents, for their unwavering belief and for not asking questions about the dubious life choices. To my best mate, Gabriel, for his constant support. To Danny A and David C, whose enthusiasm for this book made completing it a genuine pleasure.

To those brave souls who survived early drafts, kindly pointed out every stupid, embarrassing, or head-scratching moment, or expertly pretended not to notice the growing gin collection on my desk: thank you. Your brutal honesty and steady encouragement made this story sharper than I could have managed alone.

To the readers who picked up this blood-soaked, blade-swinging, chaos-laced novella and said, 'Yes, this is exactly what I need,' you're the real champions. Your enthusiasm fuels every reckless character and every twist that makes no sense until it does.

And finally, to the friends and foes who unknowingly lent their quirks, flaws, and occasional bad habits to these characters: my sincerest apologies and deepest thanks. You know who you are—and yes, you definitely did this to me.

Here's to all of you—for keeping the chaos alive, one page (and questionable decision) at a time.

ABOUT THE AUTHOR

Cassian R. Rowe writes bold, character-driven fiction where fantasy tangles with sci-fi, mystery coils in the shadows, and pleasure is always near—usually with a blade, a secret, or a skillfully placed, silver tongue. His stories flirt with danger and dive into desire, where intimacy cuts as deep as betrayal and heroes bruise beautifully, inside and out.

Whether it's a cursed relic, a locked vault, or a rival with a voice like smoke and fingers made for sin, Cassian's characters always find trouble—and occasionally each other—in places they were never meant to go.

When not plotting doomed heists, unsanctioned encounters, or extremely poor decisions with excellent chemistry, he's likely muttering about sleep deprivation, rewriting delightfully sinful things into sentences, or drinking too many cocktails he can't pronounce. He also keeps a weary eye on the kettle, as he's often chasing the last drop of strong black tea to fuel his terrible habits.

He lives somewhere between fantasy and noir, temptation and ruin. You'll know him when you meet him—and gods help you if he speaks.

♦

...Adanion ducked just as a fragment of ceiling tumbled past his ear, leaving a cloud of dust that smelled faintly of burnt iron.

Kril groaned from somewhere behind him. 'Next time, we pick the quiet ruin,' he muttered, wiping soot from his face.

Adanion rolled his eyes, brushing ash from his sleeve. 'Quiet ruins are boring. Where's the fun in that?'

Rhazha peeked over a toppled pillar, her grin sharper than any blade. 'Chaos, on the other hand...' The phrase was left unfinished, her eyes glinting with mischief.

'Tharen darinin laru li voran shovar,' Adanion murmured,
letting his words hang in the smoke.
(THAH-ren dah-ree-NEEN lah-roo lee VOH-ran SHOH-var)

'The cleverest fools make the loudest chaos.'

Somewhere above, the stars twinkled, as if laughing with them—or at them. Probably at them.

ALSO BY CASSIAN R. ROWE

Ghosts of Eidolon
The Storm of Sleepy Hollow
Orion's Phantom *(forthcoming)*
The Collected Tales of Cassian R. Rowe *(forthcoming)*